D0041720

Also by Jim Lehrer

Viva Max!
We Were Dreamers
Kick the Can
Crown Oklahoma
The Sooner Spy
Lost and Found
Short List
A Bus of My Own
Blue Hearts
Fine Lines
The Last Debate
White Widow

PURPLE DOTS

PURP

A NOVEL BY Jim Lehrer

RANDOM HOUSE · NEW YORK

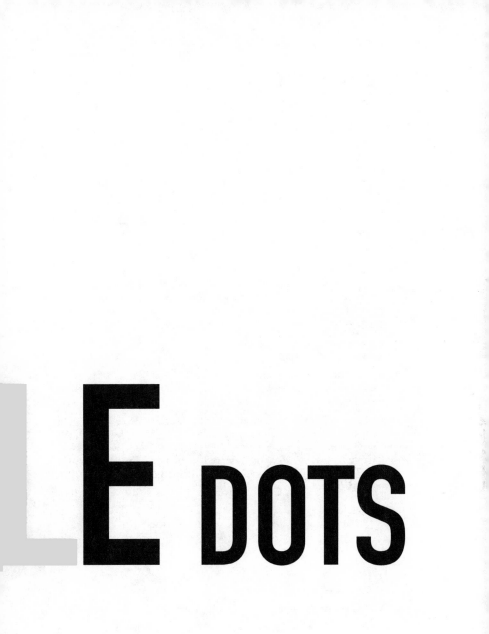

Grateful acknowledgment is made to Warner Bros. Publications U.S., Inc., for permission to reprint an excerpt from "Ev'ry Time We Say Goodbye" by Cole Porter. Copyright © 1944 (Renewed) by Chappell & Co. All rights reserved. Reprinted by permission of Warner Bros. Publications U.S., Inc., Miami, Florida 33014.

Library of Congress Cataloging-in-Publication Data

Lehrer, James.
    Purple dots : a novel / Jim Lehrer. — 1st ed.
      p.   cm.
    ISBN 0-679-45237-0 (acid-free paper)
    I. Title.
  PS3562.E4419P87   1998
  813'.54—dc21   98-12962

Website address: www.randomhouse.com

Printed in the United States of America on acid-free paper

DESIGN BY MERCEDES EVERETT

98765432

First Edition

To Ian, Malcolm and Lew

PART 1

CHARLIE

October

ONE

Charlie had not been enjoying *The Washington Post* much lately. The screwups of the new president and his administration had made for either embarrassing or infuriating reading. But, finally, there in the top left-hand corner of the front page, was some really good news. It came with the two-column headline:

BENNETT PICKED TO HEAD CIA

AIMED AT JACKSON DAMAGE CONTROL

A presidential crony and Wall Street millionaire, Joe Phillip Jackson, had been nominated for director of Central

Intelligence. He withdrew after taking many hits about his obvious lack of qualifications to run the largest and most important intelligence agency in the world. Charlie had seen Jackson's nomination as some idiots' idea for dealing with the fallout from the Aldrich Ames treachery: What about having a director who not only knows nothing about the Agency or intelligence but also knows nothing about anything else except making money?

But now the idiots had come to their senses. Joshua Eugene Bennett was the current deputy director of Central Intelligence and a friend of Charlie's. They had shared many hairy and satisfying moments in the Agency and had remained friends since Charlie's retirement. Josh, fifteen years younger than Charlie, had continued to rise through the ranks because he was one of the few good ones who had managed to escape damage from both the Iran-Contra and the Ames debacles.

Charlie—Charles Avenue Henderson—was sitting at the breakfast table at Hillmont, the eighteenth-century West Virginia manse he and his wife, Mary Jane, operated as an upscale bed-and-breakfast. He was reading the *Post* as slowly and deliberately as he pleased, which was one of the daily joys of his retirement.

Another was acting silly whenever the spirit so moved him. That spirit was about to so move him again.

Charlie and Mary Jane Henderson may have had birth dates that proclaimed them to be in their late sixties but nothing else about them did. Both maintained a spring in their steps and voices and states of mind—they could pass for early fifties, maybe even younger. Mary Jane, five feet five, with a compact figure and short gray hair, was in trim, in motion and always at the ready. Charlie, who was six feet tall, generated the same let's-go feeling. He had no paunch and no extra chins; only the thinness of his graying brown hair showed any signs of his proper age.

Charlie, also, was a Po Chü-i believer. The ninth-century Chinese poet had written some words, passed on to Charlie on his sixtieth birthday, that had become the creed for his retirement life. Po said in his poem that during a man's thirties and forties he is distracted by various lusts, and between seventy and eighty there come the ailments and ills. He ignored the fifties altogether and thus declared the good time to be between sixty and seventy.

Wrote the poet: "I have put behind me Love and Greed. I have done with Profit and Fame. I am still short of illness and decay and far from decrepit age. Strength of limb I still possess to see the rivers and hills. Still my heart has spirit enough to listen to flutes and strings. At leisure I open new wine and taste several cups; drunken I recall old poems and sing a whole volume."

Mary Jane sometimes saw Charlie's fondness for the words less as belief in a poetic creed than as proof that he had simply moved into his second childhood. Charlie claimed he had been lucky enough never to have had to end his first, having gone directly from high school to college to the U.S. Navy and then to the Central Intelligence Agency without missing a beat or being forced to do anything other than little-boy work.

"This is little-boy work, you know," he had said, for instance, to Josh Bennett one sunny day in Nice, France. They were sitting in an old town street café, posing as two American insurance salesmen attending a real event, New York Life's Salesmen-of-the-Year Week on the Riviera. There were two major international meetings going on in Nice then, and Langley had given them a choice of which one they wanted as cover. The other was a meeting of charismatic Catholics. No thanks to that, said Charlie and Josh. They chose the insurance group even though it meant wearing plastic name tags pinned on their loud sports shirts. Josh added his own touch by wearing a blue baseball cap with the red-and-white letter B of the Boston Red Sox on it.

"Hush," said Josh. "Our lives may be in danger."

"That is my point, little boy."

They were watching a man at the outdoor café next door, who had been identified by French intelligence as Vladimir Aronsky, a KGB dirty-works man. There was fear at Langley that Aronsky had come to Nice, where there was a large Russian émigré colony, to do harm to an elderly Russian woman who was working the émigré side of the street for the CIA.

"Look!" Charlie said to Josh.

"What should we do?"

"Nothing."

So they watched while a husky man with a beard and the dress of a dockworker inserted and removed the thin blade of a knife from Aronsky's back and then disappeared into the crowd on the street.

The Russian woman had apparently seen to her own protection. Or so it seemed.

But it was in fact something very different. It turned out Aronsky had wanted to defect to the West. A French intelligence officer in Moscow, intentionally or otherwise, got Aronsky's defection offer all screwed up and the result was a KGB setup in that Nice café. Aronsky, who thought he had been sent to Nice on a routine KGB courier mission, was waiting for somebody French who would speed him on his way to freedom and a new life. Instead, he got a knife in the back from one of his own. The old woman had nothing to do with it.

Charlie and Josh were held officially blameless and they went on quickly to other assignments for what was then called the Soviet Russia Division of the Agency. But neither ever forgot bearing joint witness to the assassination in broad daylight of a man who wanted to come over to their side.

Charlie in particular never forgot. He was the senior man present, he was the one who said, "Nothing." They should do nothing but watch.

All of this serious stuff was right there in his head twenty-five years later as he drove the two miles into town. He parked the Wagoneer at a meter on Washington Street, the main street of Charles Town, West Virginia, which was also Charlie's town. It was an unpretentious place of thirty-two hundred people, with a low-key race track and much John Brown history; Charlie felt comfortable and at home there. Today he had to pick up a new bicycle pump at Western Auto, only a block from the old courthouse where in 1859 John Brown was sentenced to hang for leading his unsuccessful antislavery insurrection at nearby Harpers Ferry. Two of the guests coming this weekend had said they wanted to ride bicycles over by the C&O Canal. The old pump had had it.

Something else that happened on that Nice assignment had also popped into his mind. Something not so serious that happened at the Nice airport as they were on their way out of town.

A bald-headed elderly woman in blue jeans and a white T-shirt with "Jesus Was a Freak, Too" written across the front in red had come running toward Charlie and Josh.

"Jesus! Jesus!" she screamed at Josh. "You said you would come again, and you did!"

She flung herself down at Josh's feet. "Praise God! Praise God! You came again! Here you are!"

Charlie moved aside to watch his friend, his fellow well-trained undercover agent for the intelligence service of the United States of America, deal with what they called in training an "unexpected event."

The woman wrapped her arms around Josh's right leg. "I came from Milwaukee! I came to find Jesus! I did! I did!"

Josh looked over at Charlie. Help me, you bastard! screamed his eyes.

Charlie shrugged. And tried his best to keep from laughing.

"I have a plane to catch," Josh said to the woman. "Please, now. I have to go."

Charlie wasn't the only one looking on. A circle of people, some fifteen or twenty travelers, taxi drivers, porters and others, had gathered for the show.

"No! No! Now I have you! I can't let you go! Jesus! Jesus! I love you, Jesus!"

Josh, a big man in good physical condition, took a large step with his left foot and attempted to pull his right foot free from the woman's tight grasp. All he managed to do was drag her a couple of feet.

"Give me something! Give me something of yours! Something sacred!"

Josh grabbed the Boston Red Sox cap off his head. He kissed the B-for-Boston and stuck the cap down firmly on the woman's bald head.

"Here, my daughter," he said in a voice worthy of a Vatican chapel. "Take this in my name. Wear it proudly."

The woman leaped to her feet, grabbed her head and the hat with both hands and ran away screaming, "Jesus gave me his hat! Look at me! Jesus gave me his hat! Praise God, praise God. Jesus gave me his hat!"

Josh and Charlie trotted ever so quickly to the Air France gate for their flight to Paris.

"We should have done the charismatic Catholics instead of the insurance thing," Charlie said ever so quietly to Josh as they boarded the plane. "You're a natural charismatic."

"You are a natural bastard," said Josh.

Charlie was given a special kick to remember this additional story on that Charles Town sidewalk twenty-five years later because he had to pass Messages from the Messiah, the local Bible-and-Christian-equipment store, on the way to Western Auto. He had walked by it hundreds of times before without giving it or the merchandise displayed in its windows even a glance. But this time a baseball cap caught his eye.

It was a white baseball cap with the red-and-blue waving-ribbon emblem of the Pepsi-Cola Company embroidered like a badge on the front. Written on the emblem in white, instead of the word "Pepsi," was the word "Jesus." Jesus, apparently, was the *real* real thing? Or was that Coke?

Charlie was very pleased with himself when he finally got back into the Wagoneer twenty minutes later. He had not only bought his bicycle pump, he had also sent by overnight Federal Express a $12.75 gift-wrapped Pepsi\Jesus hat to Joshua Eugene Bennett. The enclosed card said: "Congratulations, Natural. Take this in my name. Wear it proudly."

It was a silly thing to do. Little-boy stuff.

Charlie was looking for nothing so he saw nothing. He had no antennae extended, and no suspicions, apprehensions, hints or hunches were at play. That was why he failed to pick up as soon as he should have on the handsome young man named Marty Madigan.

Madigan hadn't called until just after three o'clock Friday afternoon. Did there by chance happen to be room for one more this weekend? he had asked Mary Jane. He said he had read an article in the *Baltimore Sun* travel section several months ago that had called a Hillmont weekend "a magical experience of superb elegance and time-machine history that is more than worth its pricey $450 price."

Mary Jane sometimes turned down such last-minute requests because she wanted to encourage people to think of Hillmont as a place for which you had to plan and reserve way ahead of time. We're not running a Holiday Inn here, you know, she explained to Charlie, who believed it was simply nuts to turn down any business.

"He had a good solid sound in his voice," Mary Jane said to Charlie in explaining why she violated her own rule this time.

Martin V. Madigan turned out to look as good and solid as he sounded. Tall as Charlie, lean, early thirties, athletic, blue-eyed, dark-brown hair worn slightly over the ears, at ease, in command, warm smile. He arrived in a four-year-old BMW 325i just before seven-thirty, and after showing him his room on the third floor, Mary Jane took him to the living room to meet Charlie and the ten other guests. They were already on their second drink. Madigan asked the waiter for some soda water over ice with a slice of lemon.

Why come to this weekend, spend all of that money, and only drink soda water? Charlie wondered. Maybe this young man is a recovering alcoholic. A religious teetotaler? Not likely. He seems too urbane, too East Coast for any of that.

Charlie was dressed in full Colonial—a burgundy frock coat, beige breeches, white leggings, a white ruffled shirt and a powdered wig with ponytail. Mary Jane, who was also wearing an eighteenth-century outfit, had ragged Charlie until he reluctantly agreed to attend all Hillmont weekend evening events in costume. You spent your whole adult life being other people for the CIA so what's the problem doing it now for your wife? was her argument. Charlie felt like a fool at first, but he had gradually grown comfortable being a Founding Father every Friday and Saturday night for cocktails and dinner.

Wes and Paul, the two young chef-caterers who did all of

the Hillmont cooking and serving, had laid out one of their typically lavish Friday-night dinners. Friday night was only coat and tie, less elegant than the big Saturday-night dinner, which was black tie, with string music in the background. But Friday night wasn't bad.

"I have never eaten anything quite so fine," said Madigan to the table. He was talking about the turtle soup amontillado. Mary Jane accepted his praise with a smile and the other people took the cue and spoke or grunted their agreement.

Mary Jane had put Madigan between two women guests, both of them there with their husbands, both of them in their late fifties or early sixties, both of them delighted to be chatted up by this attractive younger man. Charlie was seated next to one of those women, and occasionally he picked up a fragment of talk about the problems of the new administration, everyone's favorite topic of conversation even here, an hour and a half from Washington in the West Virginia Panhandle.

"Mr. Henderson, I assume you are pleased with the Bennett appointment," Madigan suddenly said to Charlie, who was sitting one woman away.

"Bennett?" Charlie said.

"The new choice for the Agency," Madigan said.

The Agency? thought Charlie. Who is this guy?

Charlie had a job to do at the end of the soup course, which was right now. He stood and tapped a fork against a glass.

Saved by the turtle soup!

"Good evening, one and all," he said. "I may look like

George Washington but I'm not. I am one of the two proprietors of this home and enterprise. The other, as you surely know by now, is the attractive woman who sits across from me. She is not George Washington either. Who we are is Mary Jane and Charlie. What we are are your host and hostess for this weekend. And in that capacity I hereby welcome you, one and all."

Charlie raised his glass of wine, a 1990 chardonnay from the nearby Piedmont Vineyard, and so did everyone else. "To a great weekend at Hillmont," he said.

Everyone else, including Madigan, joined in the toast.

"And speaking of George Washington," Charlie continued, "he did actually have a meal in this very room. It was on March 10, 1791. He stopped here to have dinner with an old friend before proceeding on down the road another two miles to spend the night at Harewood, his brother Samuel's home. We have a blown-up facsimile from Mr. Washington's diary entry for the evening that proves it happened. It's framed and on the wall of the library, where we'll be going after dinner. Charles Town, the town two miles back the other way, is named for another George brother. So we are in the middle of Washington country and we are all better off for it."

"Hear, hear," said the husband of one of two older women.

"Eat and drink well tonight, as George did before you," Charlie said before sitting down. "And again, welcome to Hillmont."

There was a quiet round of applause and waiters swept

in the fish course—pan roast of Rappahannock oysters with sweet potatoes allumettes.

The Agency? Who is this guy?

Is he Agency? Charlie, in his thirty-seven years of doing all kinds of jobs, had found answering that question to be among the most difficult. Two agents in deep cover cross paths by accident; a dangerous situation arises. How do they establish quickly and believably that they are not only on the same side, they are drawing paychecks from the same employer? There were many frightening stories about missed signals and close calls. Charlie even had a couple of his own to contribute.

Charlie turned immediately to the woman on his left, a Pittsburgh attorney in her forties, and answered her questions about this particular part of West Virginia and its role in the Civil War, as well as in the Revolutionary War and the Colonial period.

If he is Agency what is he doing here?

Charlie kept up the history conversation through the end of the oysters. Simple courtesy and good manners required him then to turn back to the woman on his right, and therefore in the direction of Madigan.

Charlie said only a few words to the woman between them before Madigan struck again.

"You and Bennett have known each other a long time, haven't you?" Madigan said.

"What is your interest in all of this?" Charlie asked.

"Yes, yes. Yes, indeed," said the woman between them.

"It's an occupational one," Madigan said.

The main course, venison noisettes with a sauce of pinot noir and lingonberries, Spätzle and glazed spring vegetables, was now before everyone.

"This is about as close as it is possible to get to authentic eighteenth-century food, to what George might actually have eaten here in 1791," Charlie said to the woman, in a voice loud enough to be heard around the table. Everyone quieted down and Charlie said to Mary Jane, "Why don't you explain?"

This was not part of their regular routine but Mary Jane loved this kind of spontaneity. So she picked up the cue and explained to all how Wes and Paul had gone to Mount Vernon and to the Library of Congress, as well as to the Jefferson County Historical Society and other local places, in search of menus and recipes from the period.

Charlie faked rapt attention.

When Mary Jane began to wind down her story, he said, "Tell them about the wines."

"Oh, yes, the wines," Mary Jane said. And she told everyone about the many high-quality vineyards in the area, particularly down the road in Loudoun County, Virginia, near Middleburg and Leesburg, where they bought the wines they would be drinking all weekend.

A couple of the guests had a few questions and the conversations stayed mostly tablewide and general throughout the main course.

It was not until the middle of the salad—field greens with Stilton cheese under a raspberry-walnut vinaigrette dressing—that the conversations went small again.

And it wasn't but a few counts later that the woman on Charlie's right asked Madigan the right question. "What is your occupation?" she said. Charlie wanted to hug her.

"You might say I work for the government," Madigan replied, a slight hint of mystery in his voice.

So. He definitely is not Agency. No Agency person would ever say anything so stupid and say it so stupidly. Real Agency overts say cleanly what they are and the coverts go cleanly to their cover identity and occupation.

"Which government?" said the woman. "Ours, I hope."

She laughed and Madigan laughed.

"I understand you and Bennett share a special interest in Jesus hats," Madigan then said to Charlie.

It hit Charlie like a rifle shot.

Without even a glance at Mary Jane, he stood up and announced: "Coffee and an ever-so-light Shenandoah Valley apple soufflé follow now in the library—we call it the Washington Room."

As Wes and Paul's waiters saw to the other guests, Charlie asked Madigan to join him for "a breath of fresh air" outside.

It was a stunningly quiet October evening. A three-quarter moon lit up the sky and the light came down through the trees like beams from many soft spotlights. This time of year—deep autumn, as it was called in West Virginia—was Charlie's favorite. He often told people that they would know he had been appointed God when all of the other eleven months became just like October.

Charlie led the way toward the barn some fifty yards behind the house.

"Who are you and what are you up to?" Charlie said to Madigan as they walked.

"I am who I said I was. Marty Madigan. I'm the chief minority counsel of the Senate Intelligence Committee."

Charlie stopped. Madigan stopped.

"Keep talking," Charlie said. "And talk fast, please."

"We are beginning our inquiries about Joshua Bennett in preparation for his confirmation hearings as director of Central Intelligence—"

"He's a great man, a great intelligence officer, right up there with Dick Helms, Leo Spivey and the other great ones. He will make a terrific DCI."

"We've been told that he almost cost you your life in West Berlin in 1971."

"You've been told a goddamn lie!"

"Would you mind telling me what happened?"

"Yes, I would mind."

"We can subpoena you, Mr. Henderson."

Charlie's heart was beating like a hammer.

It had been a long time since Charles Avenue Henderson had done physical violence to another human being with his bare hands. Had the time finally come to use the one technique he had never had occasion to use in the line of duty? Should he utilize the easiest, fastest and surest way to kill Martin V. Madigan? Should he crack the top of this man's nose with a karate chop and then, using the same hand in a quick follow-up move, push the nose-bone fragments up into his brain?

Or should you calm down, Henderson?

He said to Madigan, "You are now going to march back

into that house, go right up to your room, gather up your belongings, come right back down, tell my wife you have a bad case of the stomach flu, climb into your Republican car and drive your filthy young butt out of here and out of my sight before I do something that will make both of us sorry."

Madigan shrugged. "We will meet again, Mr. Henderson."

"You can count on it, friend," Charlie said with a bravado that exhilarated him.

"You make that sound like a threat."

"Take it any way it fits, Mr. Madigan."

Charlie decided to call Josh from the pay phone at the Handi-Mart down the road from Hillmont. In addition to having security concerns, he did not want to alarm Mary Jane, who was already upset enough about Madigan's sudden departure. She had not bought the story about a stomach flu. Wes and Paul had prepared one of Charlie's favorite breakfast feasts—yellow grits with white cheddar cheese, pheasant sausages, homemade cinnamon buns that were out of this world and three kinds of fresh fruit juices.

Josh was already at his office at Langley when Charlie got him on the phone. Saturday morning was just another work morning for most of the higher officials of the Agency. It was part of the culture.

"Let's do this on the egg machine," Charlie said.

"Hey, Charlie, come on. Ain't nobody here but us chickens."

"Goddamn it, Josh, put us on the egg machine!"

The "egg machine" was the secure-communications system that scrambled telephone conversations for everyone except the two parties doing the talking.

It took Josh only a few seconds to get the call switched over.

Charlie told him about Madigan.

"I know him," Josh said. "He's harmless."

"Why, then, are the Republicans fishing for dirt, Josh?"

"Let 'em fish. There is none."

"Yes, but why are they looking?"

"I'm in great shape with all of the Republican senators on the committee. Madigan is freelancing or something. He's nothing. I promise, Charlie."

"He knew about our Jesus thing, Josh."

"I loved the hat, by the way. I should have mentioned that earlier . . ."

"Did you tell a lot of people about the hat and what it all meant, the stuff in Nice and all of that?"

There were a couple beats of silence. Then Josh said, "No. The hat just came yesterday."

"Think about it, Josh. Think about how Madigan knew about it."

"Charlie, your imagination is on the loose."

"Somebody right there on the seventh floor is feeding information to somebody on the outside."

"Not necessarily."

"He also knew about West Berlin and the Czech."

"Nobody should know about that."

"Exactly. Nobody but somebody with access to a lot of our old secrets. Nobody but somebody with harming you on his mind."

That drew another couple of beats of silence.

"Charlie, every source, private and public, tells me there are no nobodies or somebodies on the committee who are opposed to my nomination. They have all concluded that a clean career man is better than an outsider after all. Everything we have points to a unanimous vote for confirmation. They're even talking about a unanimous voice vote when it goes to the full Senate."

"Then how do you explain Madigan?"

"I can't. But I will look into it. It's got to be absolutely nothing."

"It doesn't have to be anything of the kind, Josh, and you know it."

TWO

It was Monday afternoon, the guests from another unique Hillmont weekend were gone and Charlie and Mary Jane were in the Wagoneer on the way to Harpers Ferry to have a look at a milk truck and a stuffed deer head.

Harpers Ferry, ten miles east of Charles Town, was where the Potomac and Shenandoah Rivers came together, and where John Brown was captured after having led his band of revolutionaries against a federal armory in 1859. Now its few two-story wooden downtown buildings were preserved and opened to the public as a small place of history by the U.S. Park Service.

"What happened between you and that charming young man Friday night?" Mary Jane said. Charlie knew she would eventually get around to it. She always eventually got around to everything.

"Nothing worth talking about," Charlie said.

"I saw him go outside with you and five minutes later he's packing up and gone. That's worth talking about."

"He made a pass."

"No! He was a homosexual?"

"It was a national security pass."

"You promised there'd be no more of that kind of playing around."

Charlie smiled at that. He never promised anything of the kind and she knew he never would—but she would also never give up trying.

"Was he Agency? You're not up to something with them again are you, Charlie?"

"You know I'm too old for that."

That was what Charlie always said but did not mean—or practice. He enjoyed the occasional opportunities that had come his way since retirement to play around with his old friends and colleagues. They helped keep alive the Po Chü-i spirit that held back any possible feeling that he was a discard, used, over.

And here he was again. What Mary Jane did not know was that their short ride to Harpers Ferry was not as routine and innocent as it appeared.

Charlie had gotten a call shortly after one in the afternoon from Sam Holt, owner and operator of Rosebud Sam's

Antique Toys and one of many former Agency people who lived in and around the West Virginia Panhandle. Sam was an expert on Soviet history, art and culture who became one of the Agency's premier interrogators. He had spent most of his career debriefing Soviet defectors, as well as agents like Charlie. But he was occasionally sent on special assignments, and it was on one of those that Charlie and Josh got to know him.

"Your Ralston shipment has arrived," he said to Charlie on the phone from Harpers Ferry.

"What shipment? Ralston?" Charlie said. "I didn't order anything . . ."

"Let's try that again, Charlie. Your Ralston shipment has arrived. Now think and think and think way, way, *way* back."

Think and think and think way, way, *way* back.

"Take a tip from Tom," Sam said in a lyrical way that came close to singing. "Go and tell your mom . . ."

That did it.

"I always loved Shredded Ralston," Charlie said.

"Tom knows that and he salutes you for it."

Charlie then knew everything. He told Mary Jane he was going to run over to Harpers Ferry to look at a 1940s tin-plate milk truck from a dairy in Kansas City Sam Holt had just picked up at an antique-toy show in Gaithersburg, Maryland. Charlie was not obsessive about it, but he did have two small cast-irons, the beginnings of a modest collection of toy milk trucks. He had started it because of his fond memories of riding the routes with his late uncle Walt, who had been a milkman in a suburb of St. Louis. Mary Jane made him keep them on the top of his own dresser in their bedroom so as not to interfere with the perfect eighteenth-century motif in all other parts of the house.

"I'll go with you," she said. "Marcus says he's found a deer head that he believes once hung here at Hillmont."

"I do not want the heads of dead animals on the walls of this house," Charlie said. "They're not eighteenth-century even—"

"I don't want to buy it. I just want to see it."

Marcus was a retired curator and restorer of old houses and other structures for the National Park Service. He had helped establish the service's big restoration facility outside Harpers Ferry, and now he occasionally did consulting and brokering work for people with restoration projects.

Charlie would have preferred to go to Harpers Ferry alone, but the choice was not his.

He dropped Mary Jane at Marcus's house up on East Ridge Street by the Hilltop House hotel and then backtracked down to Sam's on Harpers Ferry's main street.

John Brown was not the only famous American associated with Harpers Ferry. Thomas Jefferson had also made a mark here. The confluence of the Potomac and the Shenandoah in a gap between hills, viewed from a rock high above it, "was worth a voyage across the Atlantic" to see, Jefferson wrote.

Sam's shop was a Harpers Ferry pleasure that appeared in no tourist guidebooks. It was mostly for grown men who still liked to play with toys. Cast-iron, tin-plate and wind-up cars, trucks, wagons, tractors, buses and trains. Lead soldiers, cowboys and Indians. Old football helmets and shoulder pads, old

baseball gloves, bats and balls. Cap pistols, rubber guns, Daisy
Red Ryder air rifles, Erector Sets, board games, handcuffs,
G-man badges, decoder rings, doctor kits, microscopes, bin-
oculars, baseball gloves, marbles and most everything else any
healthy male child growing up in the late thirties through the
fifties had ever wanted. There were even three red 1947
Cushman motorscooters for sale at five thousand dollars–plus
apiece. Just about everything in there seemed to Charlie too
expensive to buy, and as best he could tell most of the other
people who came in felt the same way. But Sam didn't seem
to mind. He seemed in the business more to possess these joys
of childhood than to sell them. The store kept no regular
hours and was open by appointment only.

"The tune, Charlie," he said immediately. "Do you remember the tune?"

"You bet. Listen to this."

Charlie, in a voice mostly unused since his childhood,
sang:

> *"Shredded Ralston for your breakfast*
> *Starts the day off shining bright;*
> *Gives you lots of cowboy energy*
> *And a flavor that's just right;*

> *"It's delicious and nutritious*
> *Made of whole grain western wheat;*
> *Take a tip from Tom,*
> *Go and tell your mom*
> *Shredded Ralston can't be beat."*

Tom, of course, was the cowboy-movie and radio star Tom Mix. The song was the advertising jingle Tom sang to open and close his weekly radio show.

"You have sung the magic words, come right this way, sir," said Sam, a small, dark, studious man who was closer in age to Josh than to Charlie. His early retirement from the Agency two years ago had surprised a lot of people. Most everyone assumed it had to do with Ames, but nothing was ever said officially. Anyone who left the Agency during that time was assumed to have done so because of some connection, no matter how obscure, to Ames. Charlie had asked Sam about his leaving once and Sam had said only, "Politics." Despite being younger, Sam was rounder than Charlie. Sam had never taken care of himself and probably never would. Charlie did not feel he knew Sam well enough to ask him why.

Charlie followed Sam to the rear of the shop toward a door marked "Inner Sanctum." Charlie had been inside before. It was an office with a desk, some file cabinets, a coffee-pot and a few chairs.

Seated in one of the chairs was a man wearing a white baseball cap with the word "Jesus" embroidered in front like a badge.

"You were right, Charlie," Josh said. "Right on target."

"This is one time I'm sorry I was right. Who are they?"

"They're from the Republican side of the committee. That's all I know. I don't know how deep and wide it goes."

"What's their problem with you?"

"I don't know."

"Don't know? Come on, Josh. Knowing things like that is the business you're in."

"I don't need to be reminded of that, Charlie. OK?"

"Sorry. What can I do to help?" Charlie asked.

"Find the answers to your first two questions."

"Who are they and what's their bitch?"

"That's right, Mr. Henderson."

Sam had left them alone in the Inner Sanctum. But Charlie knew that was an illusion. The DDCI—deputy director of Central Intelligence—is never alone. Somewhere out back or overhead or under a 1948 ten-car Lionel model of the Santa Fe Super Chief lurked three or four young men or women in dark suits with plastic earpieces in at least one ear and Uzi machine guns and/or radios in their hands.

Charlie assumed there were no electronic listening devices working the room. Josh would not be talking this openly if that was even a remote possibility. The idea of running an electronic antibug sweep of Rosebud Sam's Antique Toys shop was almost funny. Almost.

Charlie said, "Why not use some of your own people? I'm old and out of practice and I have no resources, no assets."

"I would rather have an old and out-of-practice Charlie Henderson than some of the young and in-practice types we have around now. But, as a practical matter, it's too dangerous to do this in-house anyhow."

"Why, for Christ's sake?"

Josh put his hand to his head and removed the Jesus hat.

"You were right about everything, Charlie. Whatever is going on, somebody right up there with me is involved in it."

"Got a name?"

"Most probably Russell Bushong, Esquire."

"A worthless, showboating jerk who should have been canned, fanned and tossed years ago."

"My view exactly and Bushong knows it. Booting him out of operations will be my first act as DCI and he knows that, too." The directorate of operations was where all covert activities originated, operated and ended—ended poorly under Bushong, in Charlie's opinion.

"What's the connection between Bushong and the Republicans?" Charlie asked.

"Mutual self-interest probably. I know Bushong's interest; he wants to save his job. I don't know the Republicans'."

"I'll find out, Josh," Charlie said—in a statement that was pure bravado. He had not one idea about how he might do that.

They both stood. It was time to go.

"You remembered Tom and Shredded Ralston?" Josh asked.

"It took a while but it finally came back."

It hadn't been that big a deal but it had been fun. While home on annual leave in São Paulo, the number-two guy in the Brazilian embassy in Moscow sent word through a U.S. embassy channel that he had "an access" to sell. The access was to the sister of Alexei Ustinov, one of Chairman Brezhnev's four private secretaries. Both the Brazilian and the secretary's sister were opera fanatics and had become friends through some kind of opera-support group in Moscow. The CIA station chief in São Paulo thought the whole thing might be a setup, so Josh and Charlie, joined a couple of days later by Sam Holt, were sent to São Paulo. They had a series of clandestine meetings with the Brazilian in out-of-the-way hotel rooms and safe houses. The guy was impressive—he spoke seven languages, including English with a Kennedy accent. He said he had learned English while living as a kid in Boston when his father played first viola in the Boston Symphony Orchestra. There was something in the way he talked about those kid days in the United States that didn't sound right to Charlie. Sam also pointed out that there were several platoons of KGB types who had had the same English teacher in spy school who, without realizing what he was doing, had taught them all to speak English like a Kennedy. Could this guy be one of those distinguished graduates?

Did you listen to the radio there in Boston? Charlie asked.

Yes, sir.

What programs?

Jack Armstrong, Hop Harrigan, Captain Midnight, Tom Mix— all of the good ones.

Who sponsored *Tom Mix*?

Shredded Ralston.

Do you remember the opening song?

Sure. And the guy sang it in a voice and tone and accent that could have passed for those of the great Tom Mix himself.

Charlie, Josh and Sam had all joined in by the time he got

to the ending plea: "Take a tip from Tom / Go and tell your mom / Shredded Ralston can't be beat."

And a long and fruitful Cold War relationship was born.

"Whatever happened to that Brazilian?" Charlie asked Josh as they prepared to leave the Inner Sanctum.

"Good question," Josh said. "I'll order a records sweep to find out."

They agreed on some old-fashioned tradecraft ways for each to contact the other when necessary. Then Charlie asked, "What was your cover for being up here today, by the way? This is a long way from Langley on a Monday afternoon."

"The fisheries. I'm on a routine surprise inspection trip, and while I was up this way I decided to stop in here for a look at some old toys in a shop run by an old and dear Agency friend."

The fisheries. The federal government operated a fish laboratory and experimental station in Leetown, a tiny place on a back road between Charles Town and Martinsburg. Charlie had always heard that the Agency had some kind of top-secret little facility of its own up and over a hill behind it.

"What do we . . . you do back there anyhow?" Charlie said to Josh.

"Top secret, Mr. Henderson. Top secret. You're not cleared for that anymore."

"If I save your ass from Bushong and the Republicans will you tell me?"

"Nope. But you would be getting the short end of the deal anyhow. What's involved up there is mostly silly, stupid stuff."

Josh disappeared through a rear door.

Charlie went back into the store and played for a few minutes with toy Chevys and Packards, Captain Midnight decoder rings, Nocona baseball gloves and a few other such things before he left through the front door and got on with the grown-up business at hand.

Charlie's first task was to entice Martin V. Madigan back to West Virginia. He did so by promising full disclosure about everything Madigan wanted to know.

"I had a hunch that deep down inside you had to be a good Republican, Mr. Henderson," said Madigan.

They were sitting on two Windsor chairs in a small sitting room upstairs over the Yellow Brick Bank restaurant in Shepherdstown, population twelve hundred, another of the small-town treasures of this particular part of West Virginia. The room had a curved picture window that made it possible to look west down German Street, Shepherdstown's main street. Kevin Connell, the owner of Yellow Brick, was a friend of Charlie's, but more important for this operation, he was an even better friend of Jay Buckner's.

Bucker was a former Agency man who now sold real estate here in the Panhandle, a narrow strip of West Virginia stuck between Maryland and Virginia like a finger pointing east. He was the person most responsible for turning the area into a popular place for old spies to live and prosper. As a technical services man in the Agency—communications, armaments, electronics, security—he was one of the few who moved among its various compartmentalized divisions and sections. Thus he had contacts among the covert operators, such as Charlie, but he also knew the intelligence analysts, the administrators, the scientists and the others. Through them all he spread the word about the Panhandle. Come here for a quiet country life, only ninety minutes from Washington, that is cheaper and easier than life in the tony Hunt Country of Virginia near Middleburg. Come here for a lifestyle in mostly untouched places that were part of both Colonial and Civil War history.

The talk on Buckner when he was at the Agency was that his success had as much to do with his physical appearance as with his brains. He was virtually invisible. Not only was he "thin enough to slip through a keyhole," his hair—something vague between blond and brown—and his eyes—grayish— were entirely unnoticable. Equally unremarkable were his height, five nine, and his face, which was like the guy's at the grocery store checkout counter. Jay Buckner, they said, was a man made by God to be in the background.

He and Charlie had never been particularly close, or even friendly, but that was an irrelevant detail now because God had made Buckner a man skilled at bugging a room.

"All right," said Madigan, "I'm listening. What did Bennett do on that day in West Berlin? Take me through the whole thing."

"Certainly. I'll be glad to. But I would like to know first exactly what it is you and your colleagues are up to. How would my information be used and by whom?"

"The Constitution calls for the Senate of the United States to advise and consent on presidential appointees. That's what this is all about. The president has nominated your friend Bennett to be director of Central Intelligence and we are—"

Charlie had his hand up as if stopping traffic at a school crossing. "Cut the crap, Mr. Madigan. You may have time to waste but I do not."

"Yes, Mr. Henderson, I guess it must be pretty taxing dressing up like George Washington every weekend."

Charlie stood up abruptly and said, "End of clandestine meeting, end of your games, Mr. Madigan."

Still seated, Madigan replied, "You're the man of games and crap, Mr. Henderson. If you are once again throwing me out of your sight, so be it. If on the other hand, you really are interested in helping your country avoid what appears to have the potential of becoming an absolute national security catastrophe . . ."

Madigan let the sentence, the thought dangle. Charlie sat back down.

"Josh Bennett has no 'potential of becoming an absolute national security catastrophe,' " Charlie said.

"What if I told you we have information that shows Joshua Eugene Bennett to be a thief. An old-fashioned kind of thief. The kind who steals money that belongs to others— and that he has been doing it for years."

"I do not believe that."

Madigan, proving to be about as cool a fool as Charlie had ever encountered, went on: "What you believe is interesting but hardly of much importance, Mr. Henderson. What is of importance is whether you will voluntarily help the

Senate of the United States carry out its constitutionally mandated task of advising and consenting on the nomination of Joshua Bennett to be director of Central Intelligence."

Charlie said, "Please, don't make a speech. You sound as if you're delivering an opening statement of some kind."

"I was just making sure Mr. Bennett understood clearly what was happening here."

"Now what are you saying?"

"I assume an exotic Agency-developed electronic eavesdropping device has recorded everything we have said here now, and I assume this recording will be made available to Mr. Bennett. That is what I am saying. And that is all I am saying. Good-bye, Mr. Henderson." He cuffed his hands to his mouth and said off into a corner of the room, "And to you, too, Mr. Bennett."

Madigan stood and moved quickly toward the room's only door.

"Wait a minute," Charlie said.

"I have no more minutes for you, Mr. Henderson."

"Who are you working for on this, on trying to get Josh?"

"I work for the American people, Mr. Henderson."

"No American people I know, Mr. Madigan."

And after asking about the quality of the food in the restaurant below, Madigan was gone.

It had been a while since Charlie had felt such a deep, sad, sick feeling of absolute failure.

He knew for certain that he was in dire need of help from a select few of those American people he did know.

One of them was a woman named Carla L. Avery. He would talk to her on the phone later that afternoon after he returned to Hillmont. He was well aware she despised both him and Josh.

Charlie could only hope and pray that she hated Republicans even more.

Charlie set up the rendezvous for right there at Langley, in Josh's office on the seventh floor, right there for the whole world to see. He did it with an ordinary phone call from Hillmont, without the use of the egg machine. He even told Josh to make sure he had a tape player handy because there was something Charlie wanted him to hear.

Charlie was doing what he and his helpers—Sam Holt, Jay Buckner and four other former Agency people now living in the area—had agreed that he would do. They had showed up one at a time, casually and over a period of thirty minutes, at the Blue Ridge Outlet Center in Martinsburg, fifteen miles from Charles Town and, with a population of fourteen thousand, the largest town in the Panhandle. More than forty national retail stores had discount shops there in a cluster of old brick buildings that had been clothing mills in their first lives. One of the seven attendees, Bill Reynolds, was a partner in the company that operated the center. He arranged for a small secure room near the manager's office. They talked for more than an hour about what Charlie, with some help from some of the others, would do next.

And now Charlie was doing it.

Within minutes after Charlie arrived at Josh's office, they were listening to the brief tape of Madigan and Charlie in the room above the Yellow Brick Bank restaurant, discussing the character and attributes of Joshua Eugene Bennett.

"What should I do about this, Charlie?" Josh said when the last word had been spoken on the tape. He had worn the white Jesus cap while they listened. Now he removed it and placed it on the desk in front of him.

Charlie had no ready answer. He let his gaze go out the window to his left. The Potomac River was out there on the other side of the trees. So was a section of Northwest Washington. So was a whole different world from all of this here in the seventh-floor office of the deputy director of Central Intelligence. This office had been one of the most important places in Charlie's world for thirty-seven years. Now it was where a friend of his worked, a friend who had a problem. There were many things about his old life that Charlie sometimes missed, but these moments of serious contractions in the chest and throat and stomach that came with considering options and consequences were not among them. They were not a part of his postretirement playing that he enjoyed.

"I don't know how to fight this kind of thing, Charlie," Josh said. "Maybe I'll call the president and ask him to withdraw my name. I do not want to put my family or myself through the kind of hell this is clearly shaping up to be."

"No, no, Josh. You can't quit."

"Then what do I do?"

Charlie said, "You fight, you go on the offensive in a major way."

"For instance?"

"For instance, do a little friendly terrorizing."

"Charlie, no! I can't be a party to that!"

"You won't have to be a party to anything."

Charlie said his good-byes and, with the help of the building pass Josh had arranged, took the back stairs down to the sixth floor to the office of Russell Bushong, director of the operations directorate.

Charlie despised Bushong, and he despised the people who put him where he was even more. While Charlie believed intelligence was an art of action and possibility, Bushong saw it as the science of avoiding anything that might go wrong, anything that might piss somebody off, anything that might involve risk, anything that might actually accomplish something. He was like a pilot who hated to fly, a cop who was afraid of the dark, a teacher who hated kids and books. All he really cared about was having his job, not doing his job. He had been promoted up the ranks through the Agency by people who felt the same way about theirs.

The Bushongs were among the parts of his Agency life that he never missed.

"Charlie Henderson, an old man in an old place," Bushong said to Charlie, who was interested—but not surprised—that he was shown right into Bushong's office even though he had not called ahead and had no appointment.

"I was just up seeing Josh," Charlie said. "I guess you already knew that." Bushong was a tall thin man of fifty-five with no hair on his head, too much of it in his eyebrows and a reputation for loving Jaguar automobiles more than people.

He dressed as if he frequented a designer store for movie spies. Today he was in a light brown tweed suit, a red paisley bow tie and a white shirt with a button-down collar.

"I not only did not know," Bushong said, "I would not have cared if I had."

Charlie elected to get right to it. "I have been told that you are feeding information about Josh to the Republican minority of the Senate Intelligence Committee."

Bushong blanched. His deeply tanned face actually jerked to the right as if it had been hit with a fist. "Who told you that?"

"Martin V. Madigan told me that. He said you had given them everything you could find in the Agency files on Josh. That's illegal, Bushong, for one thing. A capital offense, maybe even. It's also dishonorable."

"Madigan did not say that . . ."

"He said it when the tape recorder wasn't running, Bushong. Madigan was wearing a wire, wasn't he?"

"He lied."

"If you don't back off, Bushong, some of us old men are going to see to it that you pay a very high price. Josh Bennett is a decent, honorable and qualified man."

Bushong's brown eyes, in his version of a fake sinister squint, were now almost closed. "You're going to have me killed, is that it, Henderson? That is the price I will pay? Grow up, you old fool. The cowboy days are over. Now get out of here."

Charlie got out of there. He had done what he came to do.

. . .

Mary Jane, again, had come with him. When he told her he might have to go into Washington one day soon, she said, "Great, I have scads of things to do down there."

He had dropped her at Mazza Gallerie in the middle of the Chevy Chase shopping area, where she was going to cruise through Neiman-Marcus, Lord and Taylor, Woodies, Saks and like places, before having a late-afternoon tea with Lea Steinbeck, an old Washington neighbor. Then she was going to see the big new twentieth-century sculpture exhibit at the National Gallery downtown, where Charlie was to pick her up after doing what he had to do at Langley. They would have dinner at a nice restaurant while rush hour ran its course and then drive the ninety minutes back home to West Virginia.

So now he drove the Wagoneer out of the CIA parking lot, turned in his building and parking passes to the uniformed CIA security officers at the front gate and drove the half mile out to Dolley Madison Boulevard, the main four-lane road that came off the Chain Bridge and George Washington Parkway to McLean, Langley and some of the plusher Northern Virginia suburbs.

He turned left at the traffic light, where two small white crosses on a traffic island marked the spot where a nutty Pakistani had shot and killed two CIA employees a few years earlier. He drove five blocks to the Exxon station, where he had filled up so many cars when he was with the Agency. But it wasn't gasoline he wanted this time. It was the use of one of the outside pay phones.

He dialed the number of Rosebud Sam's Antique Toys in Harpers Ferry.

"Mr. Lionel, please tell Mr. Mix to shred the Ralston," said Charlie to Sam Holt.

"Yes, sir, Mr. Jefferson," answered Sam.

Charlie had come right out and declared to Mary Jane that he wanted to eat dinner at New Heights, a small, bright, delicate place that served food to match. He did not tell her why— that it was this restaurant's proximity to another one that was important this particular night.

New Heights was near the corner of Calvert and Connecticut and two of Washington's largest and oldest hotels, the Sheraton Washington and the Omni Shoreham. Mary Jane loved the special lightness of the food and the portions at New Heights, and Charlie appreciated the view. At a window table, it was possible to look down into the trees of Rock Creek Park and watch the steady early-evening flow of cars and people.

Charlie usually resisted coming here because of the parking problem. His near-obsessive annoyance over the difficulty of finding a place to park—particularly in Washington— stemmed from several embarrassing episodes when his illegally parked CIA car was towed while he was on a discreet surveillance or some other project in behalf of freedom in the Western world. But this evening, no problem. He found a place at a meter just around the corner from the restaurant.

He ordered a black-bean pâté with smoked tomatoes in a light green-and-yellow-pepper sauce as an appetizer and a grilled venison chop with fig sausage and polenta croutons in a wild-mushroom marinade as the entrée. Mary Jane had oysters and scallops with a blue cornmeal crust and, to start with, tobiko ravioli. They had a 1993 Barboursville chardonnay to go with it. Wes had been urging them to try the Barboursvilles as a possible addition to the stock of Virginia wines they served at Hillmont. The Barboursville vineyard was located near Charlottesville, next to the remains of a mansion that Thomas Jefferson had designed for a friend. It was destroyed by fire on Christmas Day in 1884 and had been left in its ruined state ever since.

"How did it go with Josh?" Mary Jane said soon after they had had their first sip of wine.

"It went fine."

"Tell me about it, Charlie."

He had spent his career not telling Mary Jane anything at all. If it had been left to Charlie, she would never have known he worked for the CIA. It was an uncle who told her that the man she had married two years earlier wasn't really a foreign service officer in the State Department. The uncle had a friend at State who asked about a young man around the place named Charles Avenue Henderson and discovered there was no such young man around the place. The uncle told his brother, who told his daughter Mary Jane, who confronted Charlie, who confessed and explained. This tell-no-one policy was an important part of life in the Agency, and it wasn't as stupid as it might sound. People who don't know things cannot repeat them. There were several terrible stories, part of the Agency lore, about covert operators who told their wives about a particular assignment, with tragic results.

The worst case involved a guy from the China division who was suddenly told to go undercover to Hong Kong to help turn a high-ranking Chinese intelligence officer. The CIA man had to leave within hours, the day before his son's graduation from Walt Whitman High School in Bethesda. His wife was furious, they got into a shouting match about it and the agent ended up telling her where he was going and what he was going to do there. The wife, confronted that night with an angry and despondent son, tried to make the boy understand that his father really did have to leave, that his work was important. She blurted out the destination and the mission. The son went to a pre-graduation beer party at a friend's house in the Westwood section of Bethesda. He had too many beers and told a group of his fellow seniors why his dad would not be at his graduation the next day. One of those kids told a parent or an uncle or somebody, who, intentionally or otherwise, passed the information on to a person with connections to Polish intelligence. That information, according to an after-the-fact National Security Agency intercept check, was sent from the Polish embassy in Washington to the Polish embassy in what was then called Peking. A Polish intelligence officer there apparently took the information to friends in the Chinese secret police. The result was that the father of the Whitman graduate was run over and killed by a large dump truck within hours after he arrived in Peking.

It took a while to break the silence habit, but Charlie had begun to tell Mary Jane a few things since his retirement. In the course of talking about the possibility of driving to

Washington to see Josh he ended up telling her a little bit about the efforts by Madigan and the Republicans to kill Josh's nomination. There was no reason to keep it all secret.

But there was also no reason to tell her everything, particularly everything about the Blue Ridge Outlet meeting and the decisions made there.

They were eating their first courses and talking about his meeting with Josh when they and everyone else in the restaurant heard the sound of an explosion of some kind not too far away. It did not shake or rattle anything but the sound was loud enough to notice.

"What in the world was that, do you think?" Mary Jane asked. "A sonic boom, maybe?"

Charlie said, "A water main exploding. Who knows?"

"You're smiling, Charlie. Why are you smiling?"

The New Heights' bean pâté was as good as he had remembered. And Wes was right about the Barboursville.

"You and your friends could go to jail if you do something really stupid," Mary Jane said.

A waiter told Charlie he had a phone call up at the front entrance. Charlie winked at Mary Jane and went to the phone.

"Mr. Mix has shredded the Ralston," Sam Holt said to Charlie.

"Anything slop out of the bowl?"

"Not a drop."

Back at the table, Charlie kept his smile and his silence, two of the best tools available to an effective intelligence officer, even when dealing with his spouse.

Outside on the sidewalk soon after, a well-dressed young man with a piece of white paper in his hand approached Charlie.

"Are you Charles Avenue Henderson of Route Two, Charles Town, West Virginia?" the man said.

"Yeah, right . . ."

"I hereby serve you with this subpoena on behalf of the Senate of the United States. It orders you to appear at a pre-scribed time and date before duly constituted members and staff of the Senate Select Committee on Intelligence. Failure to do so would place you at risk of being deemed in con-tempt of Congress. Thank you, sir."

THREE

One of the ex-Agency types who had met with Charlie at the Blue Ridge Outlet was Jonathan Scotland (Scotty) Hartman, who at three hundred pounds and seventy-five years was the largest and oldest man in the room.

Fortunately for Charlie, Scotty was a lawyer who had spent his last fifteen working years as the Agency's general counsel. On the following Thursday morning at eleven Scotty sat next to Charlie at a conference table in a scrubbed and soundproof room on the Senate side of the U.S. Capitol in Washington.

Martin V. Madigan was one of the five men sitting directly across from Charlie and Scotty. But it was the man in the middle who was doing the talking. He was Senator Lank Simmons of New Mexico, the Senate minority whip and ranking minority member of the Senate Intelligence Committee.

"Cooperation with the Congress of the United States is a critical part of serving in the executive branch of government, Mr. Henderson," said the senator. "And the obligation continues even after retirement . . ."

"That is absolute nonsense and you know it," Scotty Hartman said. "You have a Republican colleague in this very Senate who got here because he lied through his teeth and his every other body part to the Congress of the United States, the very place in which he now serves."

"I don't think either the Honorable Oliver North or I need any lectures from a former CIA man about lying," said Simmons, whose appearance matched his roots and his politics. His face was as red-brown as the earth of New Mexico and the rest of him fitted the stereotype of the conservative— tall, thin, blond hair combed straight back, dark blue suit, white shirt, maroon tie.

"My client is here in response to a subpoena," Hartman said. "Why not ask him what you want to ask him so we can get back to West Virginia, where the air and the life are clean and fresh."

"I am running this session, Mr. Hartman."

"Then run it, Senator. For Christ's and democracy's sake, run it."

Scotty was following the agreed-on strategy. But Charlie was suddenly wondering if it was the right one. Taking on a senator as directly as this was hard on the ears—and the nerves.

Simmons said, "Hartman, if you had talked like that to me or anyone else in the Senate when you were CIA general counsel . . . well, I don't know what might have happened."

"I would have been a happy man a lot earlier in life than I was, that is what would have happened, sir. I regret so much that the happiness is coming only now, toward the end of my life, rather than at its prime."

Simmons was known in the Senate as a man who, though conservative, had once made headlines by splashing water from a drinking glass on Al Hunt of *The Wall Street Journal* after they got into a shouting match on *Meet the Press*. It was that part of the senator Charlie and Scotty were going for.

Charlie had been carefully watching Simmons's face and body movements the last few minutes. It reminded him of when he was a kid, watching thunderstorms approach Joplin, Missouri, from southeastern Kansas. Darkness and lightning and deep rumbles were everywhere in the sky then; they were everywhere now in Simmons. The brown was gone from his face, leaving nothing but the red. His brown eyes had darkened.

"Are you an explosives expert, Mr. Henderson?" he said.

"No, sir," said Charlie. "I worked on Soviet affairs."

"You should go to prison for blowing up Bushong's car!"

Bingo!

Hartman, right on cue, yelled, "My client does not blow

up cars! He runs a bed-and-breakfast in West Virginia! What is this?"

"This is a search for the truth, Mr. Hartman!"

"Like hell it is! It's a witch-hunt against a loyal, patriotic American! I will not stand for this!"

Hartman started to put his papers back in his briefcase, as if in preparation for walking out of the room.

Martin V. Madigan, speaking quietly and with much respect, said to Simmons, "Senator, I believe your meeting of the Senate subcommittee on timber cutting in the national forests is already under way."

"So what? I am not going to let this Jaguar bomber and his old spook lawyer throw their weight around the United States Senate with impunity and immunity!"

Hartman, looking down and around at his own girth, said, "There is no need to be personally offensive, Senator. Americans come in all sizes and proportions, sir."

"I meant no offense to anyone of exceptional weight," said the senator. "We have many people of that nature in our state and I know and love them as I do all other New Mexicans."

One of the other men at the table said to Senator Simmons, "The senator also has a delegation of older Americans from Roswell in his office about the Pryor prescription-drug bill."

"I always have a delegation of older Americans from Roswell in my office!" Simmons yelled.

Hartman, in all of his hugeness, stood up. It was not easy for him, and it took a while. Charlie held his breath. Careful, Scotty. Don't overdo this now.

"Where in the hell do you think you are going?" said the senator to Hartman.

"I may be fat and we may be old and retired and useless to society but we are not old and retired and useless to ourselves, our families and our communities. We are going where we are needed, where people do not scream, where matters and people are under control . . ."

"I'll have you cited for contempt of the Senate!"

"Be my guest! I already have so much contempt it is only right that it be made official!"

The moment had come. Scotty had pushed Simmons right to the point where he either went up and over the side or he backed off and away.

Simmons closed his eyes, dropped his head slightly and held it there for a few counts. Then he raised it.

"A few points, Mr. Henderson, before I move out of this room and along to matters of real importance to New Mexico and the nation," said Simmons, almost as if nothing had happened. The storm had passed?

"Yes, sir?" said Charlie.

"I was at Nora's the other night with the Bushongs when their car was destroyed. It was a frightening experience. You people believe you can terrorize people into submission. Well, let me tell you that it will not work. I am surprised Josh Bennett would have anything to do with such tactics . . ."

Charlie waited until he saw Simmons about to take a breath and then did what he was supposed to do. "Senator, may I ask *you* a question?"

Simmons clearly did not like it but he nodded.

"Why are you out to get Josh Bennett? Why are you out

to destroy a man who has done nothing other than devote his life to his country and its service?"

Charlie felt the storm rising again across the table. He pressed on.

"Senator, I know for a certain fact that Josh Bennett is qualified for the position of DCI. I know for a fact that he would operate the Agency in a way that would reflect well on the Agency and the government and the people of this country. I urge you to reconsider this attack on him."

Simmons pushed away from the table and stood up. "The Constitution requires that members of the United States Senate vigorously inquire into the qualifications and backgrounds of presidential appointees. That is all that we are about here."

"That is nonsense and you know it," Hartman said. "You are out to destroy a good man for reasons that smack of politics, pettiness and disloyalty to the United States of America."

"Disloyalty? Did you say disloyalty?"

"I said disloyalty."

Simmons turned to Madigan and said in a near-whisper, "Carry on on behalf of the committee, the Senate and the people."

"Yes, sir," he replied soberly.

And Simmons left the room, taking with him the threatening storm plus three young aides, two male and one female.

Scotty Hartman was still on his feet. Madigan said to him, "Walk out of here now with Mr. Henderson, Counselor, and I can promise you other subpoenas and citations and problems you could only imagine in your worst nightmare."

"I spent all of my adult professional life dealing with threats of various kinds, young man," said Scotty. "So did Mr. Henderson here. Neither of us is of a mind or spirit to suddenly start giving in to them at this advanced stage in our respective lives. If you have some serious business to transact, obviously, we are prepared to transact it. That is why we came all of this way this morning."

"I know from personal experience that it is only an hour and a half down here from Charles Town, West Virginia. You make it sound like it's halfway around the world."

"More than halfway, young man. Much, much more than halfway."

Scotty Hartman sat back down. Again, it was not a quick and easy happening. Charlie was struck by how old and used-up this large and ancient man really was. Watching him made Charlie feel bad about pressuring Scotty into representing him.

"You came here this morning to alienate and to antagonize Senator Simmons," Madigan said to Hartman. "It seems a strange and most unusual way to go about dealing with something so serious, so consequential."

"We will make you a deal, Mr. Madigan," said Hartman. "You tell us what you people are up to with Josh Bennett and we will tell you what we are up to with Senator Simmons."

Madigan, rapidly confirming Charlie's earlier impression that he was no fool, only smiled. The smile sent no message, except maybe that he wouldn't mind making just such an agreement if it were up to him. But maybe it was not up to him? Who then was it up to? Simmons? Bushong?

"Mr. Henderson, let's talk for a few minutes about what

happened that June in Berlin," said Madigan. "I refer, of course, to the day on which you earned your Blue Heart."

Blue Heart was the extremely private, extremely unofficial name Agency people gave to the certificates awarded to Agency personnel who were wounded in the line of duty. "Blue Heart" as in "Purple Heart." Those earned by dead agents were presented to their families. Nobody outside the Agency should know anything about the term "Blue Heart." Nobody including Madigan.

"The full story is in the files," Hartman said. "Why don't you simply get it from Bushong and read it."

"Mr. Hartman, I do not have the same boiling point as a United States senator," Madigan said. "Your attempts to provoke me, if that is your aim, will be in vain. If you really are serious about making that long, ever-so-long, trip back to the other world of West Virginia anytime soon, then why not let's dispense with the lawyer games and merely do our business?"

Now it was Scotty Hartman's turn to smile. But unlike Madigan's, his was a smile with a clear message: Get us if you can, young man.

Charlie and Josh were the only two people who knew exactly what had happened that June day in Berlin. The only other person present was Kamlova, the Czech, and he was dead.

Kamlova was a second-level Czech intelligence agent who had been caught stealing sexual favors and second-level secrets from a military attaché in the Belgian embassy in

Bonn, a city where, Western intelligence then figured, at least half of the adult population was spying for somebody other than their own country. A second-level swap was worked out: Kamlova for a Chilean businessman the Hungarians had caught with some of their secrets in a briefcase. Charlie and Josh, then part of a special operations unit that dealt with Soviet and Warsaw Pact swaps and defectors, were sent to West Berlin to handle the operation. Through a coin flip it was determined that Charlie would play the part of the official and Josh would dress and act like a chauffeur and drive the car, a dark green four-door Mercedes.

They picked up Kamlova at a prison outside West Berlin at six in the morning and then headed for Glienicker Brücke. That was the forty-foot-long green steel bridge over the Havel River between West Berlin and Potsdam that had become the favorite place for East-West spy swapping. Charlie sat in the back seat with Kamlova.

They weren't more than twenty minutes from the prison when Kamlova, a gray, creepy-looking man, announced to Charlie, "I don't want to do this."

Swappers and defectors often got cold feet at the last minute, and there was a standard operating procedure for handling them. Be rough, be direct.

"Shut up, Kamlova," Charlie said.

"I will not shut up. I do not want to do this."

"It's too late. You're bothering me."

At that moment Kamlova's right hand came sailing up from his side. There was a silver .38 revolver in the hand. Kamlova stuck the barrel in Charlie's side.

"Oh, come on, Kamlova. You can kill me and nothing changes. You're going home."

"Stop this car!" Kamlova yelled to Josh in the front seat.

"He only takes orders from me and only when I give them in either Turkish or Swedish."

Charlie felt the barrel of the shiny silver pistol sharp against a rib. "Tell him to stop this car!" Kamlova screamed.

"No way," Charlie said.

"This way maybe," Kamlova said. Charlie heard the shot and felt it in his side at the same time. It felt as if an ice pick had been plunged into him—deep, with terrific force.

Charlie grabbed for the pistol and missed. He noticed the car was no longer moving. There was another shot from somewhere else and the next thing he knew Kamlova's head, spurting blood out of the forehead like a small oil well, came crashing down into Charlie's lap.

"You all right, Charlie?" Josh asked from the front seat, his pistol, a large .45, at the ready for another blast.

"No," said Charlie. "But I'm a helluva lot better off than Kamlova. You killed the sunavabitch."

"I wish I hadn't done that. It was an accident."

Langley also wished he hadn't killed Kamlova. They sent two senior men to debrief Charlie in the U.S. Air Force Hospital at Frankfurt, where Charlie was sent for initial treatment and surgery to remove the bullet. Josh was questioned separately in West Berlin.

The questions they were both asked then were almost identical to the ones Madigan asked Charlie now.

"Where did Kamlova get the pistol?" Madigan asked.

"Don't know," Charlie replied.

"Wasn't he searched, frisked, when you picked him up at the prison?"

"Yes."

"By whom?"

"Me."

"Are you sure?"

"How could I forget something like that?"

"How could you have missed finding that pistol?"

"I have been asked that question many times and I still do not have an answer. Simple incompetence, I guess."

"Why didn't Bennett merely wound the Czech?"

"He meant to hit a shoulder. But the guy moved at the last second and the bullet hit his forehead instead."

"I don't believe you."

Scotty Hartman raised his right hand. "What you do or do not believe is an irrelevancy of the highest order, Mr. Madigan," he said. "What is relevant is how and what Mr. Henderson replies to your questions."

"You know what I think, Mr. Henderson?" said Madigan, pointedly ignoring Hartman, "I think you and Bennett invented a cover story on that June day and you have been telling it ever since. I believe serious errors were made on that day by the man the president has chosen to be director of Central Intelligence. I believe Joshua Bennett killed that defector to cover up the serious errors."

Going in, Hartman had told Charlie to follow what was always the first, second and third rule for all witnesses: Never volunteer anything. But Charlie could not resist playing the game only Hartman was supposed to play: the game of antagonizing.

"You weren't there that day, sir. I was. I know what happened. You do not. If you plan to attempt to smear Josh Bennett with this crock, I assure you the crock will split open—"

Scotty, with some annoyance at Charlie, finished his client's sentence: "And awful things will spill out all over you and your treacherous little henchmen and co-conspirators."

Madigan shook his head in what looked to Charlie like disbelief. "It is a dangerous game you people are playing on behalf of your friend."

"It is you who is playing the dangerous game, young man," Scotty said.

"Will you blow up my car, too? Is that the message, the threat? I drive a four-year-old BMW 325i rather than a Jag. I'll leave it outside a lot so your bombers won't be too inconvenienced."

"We know nothing about blowing up cars. We are old men who have put all foolish things behind us in the interest of the quiet and peaceful life in rural America in the increasingly few days we have left on this increasingly unpeaceful earth. Can we go now, please? Our train is waiting."

"You didn't come by train."

Scotty and Charlie stared right at Madigan. This young man had just made one huge mistake and created one huge hole at least the size of Scotty Hartman.

"Isn't that interesting that you know how we got here," said Scotty, his voice full of glee, driving right through the hole. "Were we tailed? Did you have an operative on behalf of the Senate of the United States of America follow us from West Virginia, shadowing our every move, recording our every sound and expression? Are we under electronic surveillance in our homes and other habitats? Are there microphones in saltshakers on tables in our favorite restaurants? Are there honing devices attached to our car and pickup bumpers and tractor windscreens? Are you checking our bank accounts and our credit and driving and medical records? Have you interviewed our neighbors and our former associates? Please, young man, what kind of government, what kind of Senate have we got here now?"

Charlie had never seen Scotty better. Old and used as he was, this large man's large mind could still rise to the occasion. And in doing so just now, Scotty actually seemed thinner and younger, as well as smarter, than he was when this little confrontation began. Charlie was nothing close to being a Christian Scientist but he did believe there was a connection between the mind and body. Here now was Scotty Hartman providing more proof.

Madigan said, "This is not a courtroom, Mr. Hartman, and I am not a jury. You are wasting your courtroom histrionics. I do have another question for Mr. Henderson, if I may?"

"You may," said Scotty, his pasty face suddenly full of color and verve.

"How well did Josh Bennett account for his travel and other business expenses when you worked together?"

Score one for Martin V. Madigan. Charlie was not ready

for this question. But he hesitated only a beat before saying "He was absolutely impeccable in his record keeping and accounting."

"He did not steal around the edges? Charge for a meal he didn't have, a trip he didn't take, a car he didn't rent?"

"He did not!"

Madigan was through. At least he closed a file folder on the table in front of him as if he were through. Then he put his hands together on top of the folder and leaned toward Charlie and Scotty. "I want to assure the two of you and all others who may be in league with you that your acts and words of intimidation will not work. I want to assure you that the proper authorities at the D.C. police department are investigating with full vigor the destruction of Bushong's car. I want to assure you that the evidence will be gathered that places you and/or others in legal jeopardy because of that illegal act, and prosecution will be pursued to its logical conclusion. In other words, the book will be thrown at you. Of that you can rest assured. There may have been a time when operatives of the Central Intelligence Agency saw themselves as a power unto themselves, an organization that was accountable to no one, no government. That is no longer the case, gentlemen. I strongly urge you and your associates to back off, to stop your illegal behavior, to assist the legitimate processes of government in determining the fitness of Joshua Bennett to be director of Central Intelligence. I urge you and your associates to quit committing acts of perjury, to quit your lies and deceptions."

Scotty Hartman took a deep breath, which seemed to increase his majesty to that of a rising mountain. "Young man," he said, "that speech is one that I suggest you run up and down the halls here and deliver to some of the truly certified liars who serve in this congressional body. The wind from the laughter such unmitigated crap would no doubt provoke would blow you right out of here. If lying was a sin, Mr. Madigan, you wouldn't be able to touch a doorknob in this building because the heat of hell would have permeated this place and everything in it."

By this time Martin V. Madigan had the look of a very confused man. Charlie figured what was going through Madigan's mind was this: Wait a minute, now. We are the ones with the power of subpoena and confirmation and humiliation. We have the law behind us. Why are these two old farts acting so cavalier, so cocky? What is this?

"Shall we go?" Scotty said to Charlie.

"This isn't over," Madigan said.

"Oh yes it is," Hartman said.

Madigan's face and body expressed an even deeper state of confusion as he watched Scotty Hartman's slow effort to stand. It was impossible to do anything except watch while Scotty Hartman, back to being the old and extremely large man that he was, moved toward standing.

It took more than two minutes to get the job done, which Charlie figured meant another two minutes for Martin V. Madigan to wonder what in the hell was going on.

Going places with Scotty Hartman was an adventure in logistics as well as histrionics and legalities. Charlie and he had driven from West Virginia in the Wagoneer instead of riding the commuter train mostly because the seats on the train were not large enough to accommodate Scotty comfortably.

Now they stopped at DeCarlo's on the way out of town for an early supper because it too was easy to get in and out of. It also had booths. Delicate chairs in delicate restaurants made Scotty nervous. "The idea of falling through one, crushing it, destroying it, does not send prohibitive fears of embarrassment through me," he explained to Charlie. "It is the fear of not being able to stand up afterward that is prohibitive."

DeCarlo's was one of Charlie's favorite Washington restaurants from the old days, so it was fine with him. It was located in the Spring Valley section of Washington, more or less on the way back to West Virginia. Lucy DeCarlo, the friendly proprietor, was off on a Venice vacation of some kind but Taraz, the manager, accommodated them by putting them in the booth farthest away from the front door and from other customers.

It had been a while since Charlie had had a full meal with Scotty. It was another form of adventure. After studying the menu in silence for nearly five minutes, Scotty ordered two salads, the house salad, with a creamy vinaigrette dressing, plus the mozzarella-and-cucumber salad. And he had a plate of the spaghetti carbonara as a "starter" and then one of Charlie's old favorites, the veal parmigiana, as the main course. Plus a bottle of good Italian red wine. Charlie, because he was driving, decided to have only iced tea to go with his house salad and linguine bolognese, a pasta with a heavy tomato-and-veal sauce.

"How many lies do you figure you told this afternoon?" Scotty asked Charlie after they settled in.

"Lies?"

"You know, lies, as in untruths. Prevarications, falsehoods, whoppers, flutter-busters." Flutter was the in-Agency name for the polygraph, the lie detector.

Charlie was not sure what Scotty was getting at. "I didn't count them."

"Do."

"Do?"

"Do."

Do. Well, now, thought Charlie. On what happened in Berlin. None. On Josh and his finances. One . . . two. On the Jaguar bombing. A solid two.

"Four," he said to Scotty. "That's a conservative count."

"Four lies eyeball-to-eyeball to a United States senator and his key staff member. Think about that."

"Why?"

"Because lies are the stuff of our lives."

"Let's just eat our dinner, OK?" Charlie said.

Scotty made a big deal out of looking at his wristwatch. "It is now only five-thirty, my friend and travel companion," he said. "Only a fool would get out there in the rush-hour traffic west from this city before seven. We are not fools, are we, Charles?"

No, no. Fools definitely we are not, Charles said to himself. So relax. Relax and talk about lies.

Without any prompting Scotty said, "I am fascinated with lies, Charlie. Lies we told when we worked to protect the free world from the ravages and sins of the Communist hordes. Lies we told our bosses in the Agency. Lies they told their bosses. Lies those bosses told the president. Lies they and the president told their respective overseers in the Congress. Lies the overseers told their overseers in the press and the public. Lies the press and the public tell each other. Lies we tell our wives and children and neighbors and doctors and dentists. Have you flossed every day since I saw you last? Have you really not had a cheeseburger with fries and onion rings and a piece of German chocolate cake and a bottle of cabernet sauvignon, some port and a sambuca since I saw you last?"

"I don't consider what I did this afternoon with those clowns as real lying," Charlie said.

"Why not?"

"Because . . . well, because it was part of our strategy to save a good man from ruin."

"Lying for good purpose is not lying?"

"Lying for good purpose is lying for good purpose."

"Who decides what is a good purpose, Charlie?"

This was not the first time Charlie had had such a conversation. Louise, one of his four daughters, shared Scotty's distaste for what she called "Oliver North's lying-in-the-national-interest dodge." She first jumped Charlie about it on a weekend trip home from college several years ago. It got severe when North first ran for the United States Senate from Virginia. Charlie had no admiration for North, quite the contrary, in fact. He considered him to be a lying, self-promoting charlatan, an evil force who would use the power of rhetoric and politics to divide the country into groups of haters. But Charlie did honestly believe there were times when lies to Congress and the rest of the world could be justified.

"If I had answered Simmons's and Madigan's questions truthfully and directly, Josh Bennett would probably not be confirmed as DCI," Charlie said. "The lies I told thus were told for a good purpose as decided by you, me and our friends in that room at Martinsburg."

"Spoken, old spook friend, with almost the exact words and inflections of Oliver North," Scotty said. "They have nothing at Martinsburg that will fit me, by the way. Not a shirt, not a pair of pants, not a sweater, not a pair of shoes. I am still forced to pay full price at regular stores for my clothing and accessories. That is rank discrimination against me and my kind. I may sue somebody."

"On what grounds?"

"That it is a violation of the equal protection clause of the Constitution for Ralph Lauren, Levi's, Country Road, J. Crew and the others not to provide extra-extra-extra-large garments for customers of my size and stature. Is there such a real person as J. Crew to sue, Charlie?"

"I have no idea."

Charlie had had only a few dealings with Scotty Hartman in the Agency. Scotty was older than Charlie, for one thing, and their Agency specialities were very different, for another. But Charlie knew about Scotty—that he had gone into the Agency as a slim young undercover operator who spoke Chinese, Japanese and Thai and had roamed the Far East before ending up as an obese general counsel who roamed only as far as the end of the hall and, on occasion, as far as Capitol Hill. The unconfirmed word was that Leo Spivey, when he was DCI, thought so highly of Scotty's mind and talents that he waived all of the Agency's body-weight rules to keep Scotty on board.

"You have never asked me why I allowed myself to rise to such size and stature," Scotty said, as he moved from the pasta to the veal parmigiana. "Why haven't you asked, Charlie?"

"I consider that none of my business, that's why, Scotty."

"You just told lie number five for the day."

Charlie smiled, shook his head and took a bite of his linguine. "You are something. A human flutter, is that what you are?"

"We all are, Charlie. It goes with our territory—the territory through which we all have traveled."

Charlie said, "I remember back in the late sixties, early seventies, some kind of casual drug or something the crazies over in science and technology were working on that would cause all people to automatically tell the truth."

"Yes, yes, indeed. Think about there being a pill you could give somebody that forced the truth out of their mouths, no matter what their minds were saying or doing."

"I'd rather not think about it, thanks, particularly right now."

"Watch Sam Holt if you want to know more," Scotty said.

Watch Sam Holt if I want to know more about what?

What does that mean? Never mind, thought Charlie. He said, "Why are you fat, Scotty? That is the question I have not asked that you were about to answer."

"Yes, yes, indeed. There is no answer. One day I ate one pound of food and gained five pounds. The next day it was two of food, six of weight. And so on. It was if I were a balloon and God was blowing wind into my insides. Only it wasn't wind, it was fat and there wasn't much I could do about it. There was something in me that was diseased. And eventually it got so bad it didn't matter how much I ate, so I decided to really enjoy myself. And enjoy myself I have."

Charlie believed there was little enjoyment ever for this fat man sitting across the table at DeCarlo's, eating and drinking enough for two, maybe three, men.

Barely two inches of Scotty's red wine was left in the bottle. Half the veal parmigiana was already gone and nothing of his pasta or the salads remained. Charlie had not been counting, but he guessed eight breadsticks and at least four slices of Italian bread had also disappeared inside Scotty Hartman since they sat down in this booth. Charlie wondered if eating oneself to death was a recognized form of suicide.

"Any second thoughts about our strategy with Simmons and Madigan?" Charlie asked.

"We decided to make them mad and suspicious and hope it caused them to do something stupid," Scotty replied. "Exterminating Bushong's Jag was a particularly delicious touch in that regard—I salute you."

Salute me? No, thought Charlie. "That was a team decision, a team effort," he said.

"One for all, all for one, yes, sir." There was not a trace of a slur or any other sign of the effect of all that wine. Scotty's clarity of mind never seemed to diminish. "You ask the second-thoughts question because you are no longer so sure, is that it, Charlie?"

"That's it, Scotty."

"I would remind you, sir, that when we met to discuss strategies and options there were no others. Either we did what we did or we did nothing."

"They are really going to come after Josh now. We definitely saw to that."

"Exactly."

"Well . . . exactly, sure. What if they're smarter than we think they are in going after him?"

"That is the one thing about which I am certain and unafraid," Scotty replied. "You're not afraid of these incompetent moths and roaches, are you, Charlie?"

"No, no, nothing like that," said Charlie, telling his sixth lie of the day, continuing to count conservatively.

Taraz, a quiet man who had come to the United States from Iran after the fall of the shah, was suddenly standing there by Charlie.

"Mr. Henderson, I am sorry to interrupt, but there is a call for you back in our office," he said.

A call? For me? Nobody knows I'm here.

Charlie followed Taraz to the other side of the restaurant, past the restrooms, to a door marked "Office."

Taraz, using a key, opened the door for him. Behind a desk sat a man dressed in a tuxedo and a white baseball cap with the word "Jesus" on its front.

.   .   .

"Who had the stupid wall-banging idea of blowing up Bushong's Jag?" Josh said. They were his first words after the door was closed behind Charlie.

"I don't know what you're talking about, Josh," Charlie said. "The hat still looks good on you."

"Spare me the deniability crap, Charlie. Bushong thinks I was behind it. So does Simmons and that up-and-comer Madigan. They think I go around bombing people's cars, Charlie. They really wonder seriously now if the United States of America should have its intelligence service run by some nut who bombs people's Jaguars. And I think they might have a point. They really have a reason now to go after me. I don't know what you and your fellow old farts were thinking about but you have screwed me up. I'm thinking I might really ask the president to withdraw my name. I'll come down with some dreaded disease and cite health reasons."

The office was very small. There were stacks of paper on the desk and photos of celebrities on the walls. Charlie took the only other chair, which was directly across the desk from Josh.

"Don't quit, Josh. The country needs you in that job."

"Well, the country is not going to get me. Not if friends like you continue to blow up cars."

"We had to get their attention."

"You got it."

"I was interviewed this afternoon by Simmons and Madigan," Charlie said.

"I know," Josh said.

"Do you also know what they asked me?"

"West Berlin? The Czech?"

"Right."

"What did you tell them?"

"I told them the truth."

"Good."

"They also asked about your expense money."

"What did you tell them?"

"Nothing."

"Good."

"Might they have something else about money?"

"Not really."

"What does that mean?"

"It means, I hope not."

Charlie had nothing else to say. He let his eyes drift to the left, to a framed black-and-white photograph of Lucy De-Carlo with Joni James, the famous singer of the 1950s, who Charlie knew came often to DeCarlo's when visiting some good friends in Washington.

Josh said finally, "Please, Charlie, I really do appreciate what all you and my other old friends are doing to help me. What I asked you to do was find out why Simmons and the others are out to get me. I did not ask you to blow up Bushong's Jaguar. I have never been in the company of an angrier man than he was the next morning. If he'd thought he could get away with it he would have sprayed me with an Uzi right there in my office. The first murder on the seventh floor of the headquarters of the Central Intelligence Agency."

"That's the point, of course, Josh. We want Bushong or one of the others to try something stupid like that."

Josh broke into a very wide smile. "Stir 'em up, panic 'em, cause them to do something stupid. That's the old strategy, huh? Well, so far the only people who have done anything stupid are the guys on my side. No more bombs, Charlie. No more funny stuff, OK? The hearings are about to begin. Can I have your promise that you guys will back off? I would still like to know what's behind all of this. But that's all."

"We don't have anything yet on motives," Charlie said.

"I understand. Can I have your word on the other?" Josh stood up. So did Charlie.

"Where are you going in your tuxedo, Mr. Director-Designate?" Charlie asked, pointedly not answering Josh's question.

"To a prehearings dinner in my honor at the Metropolitan Club, cohosted by the Democratic chairman and the Republican vice chairman of the Senate Select Committee on Intelligence."

Charlie was stunned. "You mean Simmons?"

"I mean Simmons."

"Jesus, Josh! How can the same sunavabitch who is working his ass off to defame and destroy you cohost a dinner for you?"

"It's called life in Washington, Charlie."

Scotty was sipping on a clear sambuca when Charlie rejoined him in the booth. Sambuca, in Charlie's view the best of the

Italian liqueurs, came in a clear and a dark version, although the licorice taste was essentially the same in both. At De-Carlo's they also followed the Italian good-luck custom of floating three black coffee beans in the glass.

Charlie saw that Scotty was having trouble raising the small liqueur glass to his mouth.

"I told them you were driving," Scotty said, pointing to the cup of coffee that sat at Charlie's place at the table. "How was Josh?"

Charlie noticed that the words were coming slowly out of Scotty's mouth. His eyes were flicking shut and open, shut and open, as if a bright light were shining in his face. The color of his skin seemed to have changed, from pasty olive to pasty white.

Charlie said, "You set this up with Josh, didn't you?"

"Lies, Charlie? How many lies did you tell him?"

"Lies?"

"Yes, yes. You know, lies, as in untruths. Prevarications, falsehoods, whoppers, flutter-busters."

Charlie took a sip of his coffee, which was already luke-warm, and silently counted. One . . . two.

He was about to say only two when Scotty's eyes closed again, but this time they did not flick back open.

His large body slumped forward and the glass of sambuca dropped from his right hand onto the table.

FOUR

The funeral and other departure arrangements were made by his former Agency friends and other friends in the area. That was because Scotty Hartman had had three wives in the course of his life but had none at the end of it. Nor were there children from any of his marriages, and his parents and his only brother and everyone else related to him had, as they said in the newspaper obituaries, preceded him in death.

Despite Scotty's lack of any church affiliation, his friends arranged for the funeral service to be held in the sanctuary of the Zion Episcopal Church in Charles Town. Zion had roots back to the Washington family, many of whom were buried in the graveyard that surrounded the church. The ruins of the original eighteenth-century chapel were still there on a road a couple of miles west of town. The place was said to be haunted by the ghosts of young brides forsaken on their wedding days and by the spirits of many of the nation's Founding Fathers who came there to ask for guidance.

It was a magnificent day of deep autumn. There was orange in the trees and on the ground. The temperature was in the seventies; the air smelled of cedar and burning leaves. For Charlie, this day would trigger football dreams and memories of his Missouri childhood. It was a perfect example of Indian summer.

The music, played on the cello by Gene Duckworth, also had a warm autumn quality to it. Gene had been Scotty's best friend among the retireds. After he left the Agency and moved to a mountain on Antietam Creek east of Sharpsburg, Gene became the principal cellist in the Maryland Symphony Orchestra at Hagerstown. Scotty had seldom missed a performance of the seventy-player orchestra, which had been founded fourteen years earlier by Maestro Barry Tuckwell, the world's best French horn player, and was still conducted by him. Being a cellist had been Gene's cover while in the Agency's clandestine service, and he and Tuckwell had crossed musical paths many times and in many places throughout the world. The last time was when Gene turned up one day for an audition for one of the eight cellist spots in the new Maryland orchestra. The big joke between them and among their friends was the fact that both of these men of music had small goatees. Beards and music they shared, but Charlie doubted that Tuckwell or anyone else in the orchestra knew even now that their principal cellist had once been an intelligence agent.

Gene sat in a chair in front of the altar, his big cello between his legs. Charlie didn't pay that much attention to the music when he first entered the church and took a seat. Then he picked up on the sound of something startlingly familiar. It was "Ev'ry Time We Say Goodbye" by Cole Porter. Charlie knew some of the words. "Ev'ry time we say goodbye, I die a little / Ev'ry time we say goodbye, I wonder why a little . . ." Yes, yes. Scotty was a huge fan of Cole Porter's music.

Charlie did a couple of quick looks around. All of the old Agency types from the neighborhood were there. The group that Charlie had put together to work with him on the Josh problem and several others had come to pay their last respects to their former colleague. There were a few younger men in suits who looked very much out of place. Charlie thought they were probably members of the Madigan-Bushong team. He would get Jay Buckner to check them out. Jay, dressed in a navy-blue blazer and charcoal slacks, was sitting in a pew at the back.

Then Charlie saw Carla. Carla Louise Avery. What in the hell was she doing there? She left the Agency with a well-known loathing for it and the men who ran and worked in it. Did she have some past work relationship with Scotty? Was she working for Bushong and Madigan?

A middle-aged man came down the aisle carrying Scotty

in a jar. The jar—an urn—was covered by a white silk cloth. The man put the jar down on a small table in front of the altar. Charlie recognized the man as the owner of the area's leading funeral home and crematorium. It seemed unjust that a man the physical and mental size of Jonathan Scotland Hartman had been reduced to mere ashes in a jar.

Charlie hated himself for thinking about how many of this man's helpers it must have taken to get the full remains of Jonathan Scotland Hartman into the crematorium oven. Tote that man, lift that corpse . . . No, that was Jerome Kern, not Cole Porter.

The minister, a balding young man in a clerical collar and a purple robe, came out from somewhere behind the altar. Charlie had met him a few times at other funerals and functions. He read a few Scriptures, led everyone in singing "Bringing in the Sheaves" and then turned the program over to Sam Holt, who also appeared from beyond the altar somewhere. Sam, the antique-toys man, had been revered in the Agency for his exceptional skill as an interrogator. He could make dead men talk, they said. He was suitably dressed today in a black suit that matched his black hair, plus a white shirt and a deep wine-colored tie.

It was the second time Charlie had seen Sam that day. The first time also involved his coming out from behind something somewhere.

Charlie had been driving the Wagoneer in the early morning semidarkness on the back road to Shepherdstown after having sprung up and awake at five o'clock.

"I'm going for the *Times*," he whispered to Mary Jane

after he had dressed and was pointed toward the door. Mary Jane was barely awake, but she seemed to understand and not mind. She puckered her lips as if to kiss him and turned over and went back to sleep.

Thinking about Scotty's death and funeral had helped keep Charlie awake with thoughts about his own mortality. He had reached the age now when it was no longer possible to deny the simple fact that he, too, was going to die. He had spent most of his life vowing never to do it.

The Washington Post, not *The New York Times,* was Charlie's newspaper. Unless he was traveling, he read the *Post* every day, without fail, no matter what. A young man from Charles Town delivered it to the Hillmont driveway before six every morning. The only way to get the *Times* on the morning it came out was to drive twenty minutes to Ruth's Café and Pie Shop in Shepherdstown before six o'clock. For reasons that were not clear to Charlie, seven copies of the *Times* were delivered to Ruth's every morning by somebody who drove a truck down from Hagerstown, Maryland. They were sold on a first-come basis, which meant all seven were usually gone by six-fifteen. Charlie wasn't as avid a fan of the *Times* as he was of the *Post,* but occasionally he enjoyed seeing it. So sometimes when he was up earlier than usual he would make the trip to Ruth's.

It was just as he was approaching the single traffic light in the tiny town of Kearneysville that the most important event of this particular trip happened. The light was at the intersection of two double-lane blacktop roads, the four corners consisting of a twenty-four-hour convenience store/service station, a small modern brick building that housed a branch bank, an old one-story white frame Presbyterian church and an open field overgrown with head-high, uncut weeds. Little bits of town and country, old and new, needed and ignored— all connected by a traffic signal.

The light was red so he was braking to a stop. A dark four-door sedan came from the south, from Charlie's right, on the green light, and turned left, crossing in front of him. The Wagoneer's headlights caught the driver's face clearly. It was the face of Sam Holt, proprietor of Rosebud Sam's Antique Toys.

What in the hell was Sam doing on this road at that time of morning?

What was it Scotty had said at DeCarlo's? Watch Sam Holt if you want to know more.

Without thinking about it another second, Charlie did a fast U-turn and headed back down the way he had just come. In a few moments he picked up the rear lights on Sam Holt's car some fifty yards ahead.

Charlie slowed down to keep some distance. There were no other cars on the road, going in either direction.

It took less than five minutes for Sam Holt's dark sedan to reach its destination. It was the dirt road just this side of the national fisheries complex that reportedly led up and back to that supersecret facility of the Central Intelligence Agency that Josh had said he would never tell Charlie about.

Charlie drove slowly by just in time to see Sam's car moving along the dirt road up and over and then behind a small hill as if it were a comfortable and natural thing to do.

Now, barely five hours later, Sam was giving Scotty Hartman a first-rate eulogy. His best lines were: "No one who knew—or even met—Scotty will ever forget him. To say that he was unforgettable is comparable to saying the tallest tree in the forest is tall, the tiniest pebble on the beach is small, the best steak is served rare, the best Pinot Noirs come from Burgundy, the best cigarettes in the world are Gauloises."

Amen, thought Charlie. Amen.

Taraz and the others at DeCarlo's had moved quickly when they saw Scotty crumble and fall forward in the booth. Within a few minutes a District of Columbia emergency unit was there. Two men in blue uniforms beat on Scotty's chest and stuck an oxygen contraption on his face, but Charlie knew enough to see that Scotty was gone. An emergency-room doctor at nearby Georgetown University Medical Center made it official within fifteen minutes after his arrival there. An autopsy confirmed that death had been from natural causes, that Scotty's heart had chosen that moment with the sambuca and the three good-luck coffee beans to naturally stop beating.

Charlie felt more than sadness over the death of a friend. He also felt some guilt about having contributed to its cause by rousing Scotty to represent him before the jackals of the Senate intelligence committee minority. There was some solace in remembering the way Scotty had come back strong those few minutes of sparring with Simmons and Madigan. He died after a damned good last performance.

Gene Duckworth's music helped Charlie's thoughts. The sound of the cello was as deep and wide as Scotty and there was an embracing inclusiveness about it. Here we are to-gether with Scotty listening to something that sounds like Bach. Then, here we are together with Scotty enjoying Cole Porter and, finally, at the end of the service, "The Battle Hymn of the Republic." Charlie had never imagined, much less heard, that wonderful song played this way. He knew he would never forget the few moments of that sound, of that experience. My God, who would have thought a lone cello could produce such a stirring affirmation of the glory of the coming of the Lord.

On the way out of the church, Charlie talked briefly to Jay Buckner about the unknown suits among the mourners. And then he sought out Carla Avery. He caught up with her at the churchyard gate.

"Good to see you in person, Carla," he said, an unspoken reference to his phone call to her a few days earlier. "It's been a while."

"True, Charlie," she replied. True indeed. She, like Char-lie and Scotty and the others, had come to West Virginia after retiring from the Agency, but unlike most of the others, she maintained little or no contact with the rest of them—or so Charlie had thought.

"What are you doing here, Carla?" Charlie asked.

"Scotty always treated me well," she replied, leaving no doubt that she would not say the same about Charlie.

"Did Madigan contact you?" he asked.

She said nothing but her dismissive wave as she walked away said plenty. Charlie immediately put her on the agenda for tonight. Charlie and his seven—now only six—colleagues were set to meet this evening at Juan Galinda's auto-and-truck-restoration garage in Inwood.

Charlie did not know what he was going to do about his early-morning sighting of Sam Holt. He decided, there at the end of the funeral, to say nothing to Sam. Not yet.

Jay Buckner began the meeting by confirming what Charlie had suspected. The young strays in suits at the funeral worked for Bushong and/or Madigan. Then Juan Galinda gave the first report. His assignment was Senator Lank Simmons of New Mexico.

"Lank, believe it or not for starters, is the sunavabitch's real name. His father was a deputy sheriff, his mother was a waitress. They named their first and only son Lank out of hope he'd turn out that way and their hope came true. He's six five and as skinny as I used to be."

Juan, the son of illegal immigrants, had left the grapefruit fields of the Texas Rio Grande Valley to work his way through college and become a psychologist. Now in his late sixties and slightly overweight, he had been pencil thin thirty years ago when Charlie first met him. Juan specialized in the investigation, study and profiling of foreign leaders for the Agency's intelligence-analysis division, what some of Charlie's covert warrior colleagues referred to as the "Charmin" side of the operation. "Charmin" as in squeezably soft toilet paper. Charlie had seen him several times since he'd moved to Inwood, eleven miles west of Hillmont, and opened up his restoration garage. Charlie asked what the connection was between psychological profiles and restoring 1929 Ford pick-ups, and Juan said, None and isn't that wonderful?

"What kind of restaurant did Lank's mother waitress for?" Gene Duckworth asked. Gene, the traveling cellist with a goatee, had made his reputation as a recruiter of operatives from among the music-loving leaders and agents of Hungarian, Polish and Czech governments. He was known within the Agency for his insistence on having minute details about recruiting targets.

"A hotel coffee shop in downtown Alamogordo," said Galinda. "She was paid two dollars an hour plus tips and a uniform when she took the job in 1947."

"Was she happy as a waitress?" Gene asked.

"At first she felt as if she was part of the servant class, if that's what you're asking—"

Charlie stopped him. He said, "Please, will the two of you stop showing off? We're here for some serious purposes tonight."

Yes, indeed they were. But a casual observer stumbling across them might have been excused for not thinking so. Galinda had set up folding chairs around a circular table in the back of a long, wide 1941 Rainbow bread-route truck he was restoring to its earlier glory for a wealthy bakery owner in Harrisburg, Pennsylvania. The truck was sitting on concrete blocks in the center of Juan's large, locked and spotless garage.

The six other men, except for Sam Holt, were mostly Charlie's age and kind. The predominate hair color was gray or graying. Several had lost their hair; a few, like Galinda, had gained stomachs; all wore various forms of sport coats and

slacks, loafers and open-collar sports shirts or sweaters—
purchased, no doubt, from Ralph Lauren, J. Crew or one of
the other outlet stores at Martinsburg. A few were still dressed
up from the funeral. One, despite the lack of ventilation,
smoked cigarettes. Another mouthed but did not light a pipe.
All seemed anxious to do their business and get on home or
wherever they spent the evenings of their retirement.

Sam Holt, the toy man, about fifty-five and thus the
youngest of them, was the one with the pipe. Charlie had exchanged a few pleasantries with him when they arrived but
he had said nothing about the early-morning drive down the
fisheries road, not having decided what, if anything, he was
going to do about that.

Galinda continued his report on Simmons:

"He did fine in the public schools of Alamogordo. He
was president of his high school student body, captained his
football and basketball teams, got nobody knocked up and
went to undergraduate and law schools on scholarships to the
University of New Mexico at Albuquerque. He came back
to Alamogordo after avoiding the service and Vietnam because of a sinus problem and went into local politics. He was
the DA, then a state senator and finally a U.S. senator, doing
what the famous political pundit Mark Shields says they all
do."

Gene, speaking for Charlie and apparently for everyone,
asked, "And what, pray tell, would that be?"

"I heard Shields say on television that Washington is the
place all high school student body presidents end up," Galinda
said.

"Madigan was president of *his* high school student council," said Jack Albertson, the man in charge of investigating Martin V. Madigan.

"So was Josh of his," said Bill Reynolds.

"Your turns will come, please," said Charlie. "Let's let Juan finish with Simmons."

Galinda had very little more to say. He had been unable to find anything in Simmons's political life—campaign contributions, opponent allegations and the like—that provided any meat. He had been married to the same woman for twenty-seven years, there was no evidence of any kind of extramarital activity and their children were four in number and relatively normal.

"What about the draft-dodging?" Sam Holt asked.

"He didn't really dodge it. His nose has a serious birth defect that gives him habitual sinus problems."

"You really believe that?"

"I read his medical reports."

"They could be fakes," Jay Buckner said.

"Come on, Jay. We're talking small-town doctors and hospitals in the small state of New Mexico, for Christ's sake."

"Why are you defending the sunavabitch?" Charlie asked.

"I'm not. I'm just giving you the facts, which was what I was asked to do. You people always had problems with the facts."

There it was again and always. The conflict between the Charmin boys and the warriors. Again and always, now and forever.

Jack Albertson was a Civil War nut who lived on a farm

outside Shepherdstown and spent most of his spare time combing open fields and yards in the area with a metal detector looking for parts of bullets, uniform buttons and other relics. He had served well but with modest distinction in the administrative side of the Agency. He spent years interviewing and checking out and evaluating potential Agency employees, experience that was useful to him now as the man charged with finding out all there was to know about Martin V. Madigan.

Albertson said: "He was born a rich boy in Westport, Connecticut, where he really was president of his high school student council. 'Tall, dark, handsome—and destined for greatness' was what was written under his high school yearbook photo. He went to Yale, got involved in conservative politics, à la Buckley, and then pushed on to get a master's in public policy at the Kennedy School at Harvard. He won most student elections in which he was a candidate. He was hired for just about every job for which he applied, including the one he has now. He is the one and only non–New Mexican Lank Simmons has ever had on any of his Senate payrolls. He is there because, in the words Simmons used to the FBI agent in the original pre-employment background check on the guy, 'Martin Madigan is the single smartest human being it has ever been my pleasure to know—present company, meaning me, included.' "

"How in the hell did you get your hands on Madigan's FBI report?" Jay Buckner asked, with much awe in his voice.

"I'm pretty sure none of us want to know the answer to that question," Gene Duckworth interjected. "Let us be satisfied with simply being impressed with the fact of the achievement."

"I wasn't going to answer anyhow," said Albertson, obviously delighted with the peer respect he had triggered.

The need to protect ways and means, sources and methods, never leaves the soul of people like us, thought Charlie. And he was suddenly very tired. His early-morning discovery and Scotty's funeral had caught up with him. He felt some aching in the calves of both legs. A slight film, almost like a mist from an atomizer, came down over his eyes. He had worn glasses for reading and close work for more than twenty years but his distance sight had always been near perfect. Now, there across the table, Albertson and Reynolds, Sam, Gene and Jay blurred. He couldn't pick up all of the detail in all of their faces.

He had to wrap this up. "Have you got anything that we can use?" he said, breaking in on Albertson.

"No. He has a perfectly normal personal life. His credit is good. As far as I am able to determine, he doesn't even have any enemies."

"Except for us," Jay said.

Gene went right to the summary point. "The message of these two reports, old gentlemen friends, is that we have nothing to throw on the fire, nothing with which to engage the other side, nothing to temper their zeal. Is that correct?"

"Right as far as Madigan is concerned," Albertson said.

"Same on Simmons, I am sorry to say," Galinda said.

"That leaves only a disinformation possibility?" asked Reynolds.

"We make up some lies—Simmons killed cats when he was a kid, Madigan wears pink pumps and nightgowns," Jay Buckner said. "No, thanks."

Even through the blur Charlie could see No, thanks in the face of everyone at that table.

"What have either of you been able to find out about why they are after Josh?" Charlie asked. "That is what Josh himself really would like to know."

Galinda and Albertson exchanged can't-help shrugs.

"Is it possible, remotely possible, that they have no ulterior motive?" Gene Duckworth asked. "Could it be that they honestly believe he's not up to the job?"

"No," Charlie said.

"Why do you say that?"

"I don't know why. It doesn't smell right."

All Charlie really knew or could smell at that moment was that he didn't want to get into a discussion about Josh, and besides, he was an old man and he was tired and he wanted to go home. He wanted to motion to Jay, let's go. Mary Jane had taken the Wagoneer to Shepherd College at Shepherdstown for a lecture by William Howard Adams, an area celebrity who was one of the world's experts on the great gardens of the world, as well the life and times of Thomas Jefferson. Charlie had gotten Jay to swing by Hillmont and pick him up.

"What else did Josh say to you?" Juan Galinda asked.

Charlie, looking right at Jay, said, "No more funny stuff. He said, No more funny stuff. No more bombed Jags, for instance."

"That's fine with me," Jay said. "Blowing up a terrific car like a Jaguar seems almost sinful anyhow."

"Depending on its ownership," Charlie said.

Sam Holt, who had been mostly silent until now, said, "No funny stuff, no real stuff, no unreal stuff. That means no stuff at all. That means we are out of stuff, and thus out of business?"

Yes, that is exactly what it means, thought Charlie. And then, his weariness caused him to blurt out: "Hey, Sam, where were you going at five-thirty this morning? That was you on the fisheries road, wasn't it?"

Not a muscle or anything else moved in Sam's face. "You have got to be seeing things, Charlie," he said. "I haven't been up that early in five years."

Sam's eyes and demeanor expressed nothing but sincerity and truthfulness. But Charlie knew that Sam Holt was the master of the sincere pose. It went with being a legendary interrogator.

Charlie also knew damned well it was Sam Holt who was driving the car that turned up that road. He was certain of it.

Sam looked away from Charlie as if nothing of consequence had just happened and said, "We still haven't heard from Bill."

Bill Reynolds had been assigned to Josh. He was to find out if there was anything in Josh's life and background, personal or professional, that made him truly vulnerable to the Simmons–Madigan crowd or anyone else trying to derail the nomination.

Reynolds, the cigarette smoker, had been a covert operator like Charlie, but his specialty had been keeping track of the international arms trade. It was among the most sensitive work the Agency did because the definition of good guys and bad guys sometimes changed overnight. The joke around Langley was that there were few soldiers anywhere in the world, on any side, whose weapons had not at one time or another passed through the covert hands of Reynolds and a few of his colleagues. Their "coverage" was complete world-wide. Now living on a farm on Highway 9 between Lees-burg, Virginia, and Charles Town, he watched over his Blue Ridge Outlet investment and raised and trained bargain-basement racehorses, one of which had actually placed third in a race at the Charles Town track a few months before.

"Josh is as clean as we all believed, before and since he became a purple-dot man," said Reynolds.

A purple-dot man? thought Charlie. What in the hell is that? He looked around at the others. Nobody else seemed not to know so he said nothing as Reynolds continued: "He's as perfect as those other two. If they're going to get him, they're going to have to make it up."

Charlie said, "Did anything turn up about money?"

"No. There were some questions asked about some of his expense reports years ago but nothing came of it. We all know about those things, I'm sure."

Charlie told Reynolds and the others about Madigan's money question and repeated what Madigan had said earlier about Josh's being a thief.

"There could have been something in high school," Reynolds said. "Josh had some kind of run-in with the school administration that almost caused him not to graduate. But nobody's talking. It could have had to do with money, who knows?"

"And who cares, for Christ's sake?" Buckner said. "They're not going to go after Josh for something he did in high school."

"Bet not a thing on such a premise, dear man of technology," said Gene Duckworth, the man of music.

"Well, they must have something really serious," Juan Galinda said. "You don't go after a presidential appointee like that without something serious in mind."

Reynolds said, "Let's face it, Josh is no perfect all-time candidate for DCI. He's no Helms or Spivey. He's clean but he's also a bit on the ordinary side."

Galinda said, "That's probably why he survived all this time—"

"I was surprised to see Carla Avery at the funeral," Charlie interrupted.

Nobody had a response.

"I called her the other day to alert her to Madigan and his people," he continued. "I was hoping—I am still hoping—that she hates Republicans more than she does us."

Again, no response.

"I have grown weary of sitting on a folding chair in the back of a bread truck," Gene said. "I move, second and so declare this meeting adjourned so I can go back to mourning Scotty some more."

He got no argument from Charlie or anybody else.

·   ·   ·

They were barely out of the parking lot behind Juan's garage.

"What's a purple-dot man?" Charlie asked Jay. They were in Buckner's almost new Toyota Camry four-door, the back seat of which was full of various kinds and sizes of real estate signs.

"I think it has something to do with being a big shot and parking."

"Big shot and parking? What in the hell does that mean?"

"All I know is that I once heard a guy on the seventh floor say that getting a purple dot was the ultimate perk," Jay said. "Ask Reynolds—he seems to know."

Charlie waited another few minutes and miles before asking what was really on his mind: "What do you know about what's going on behind the fisheries?"

Jay said, "I know I arranged the deed work for Langley. That's it, that's all I know. Greg Didden did the sale." Didden was a friend of Charlie's who ran a real estate firm in Sherpherdstown. There was much competition and no love lost between Greg and Buckner.

"What do they actually do back there behind that place?"

"I have no idea."

"I don't believe you."

Buckner, the former tech-services man, was still in his blazer from the funeral. The only addition was a blue baseball cap with "Dallas Cowboys" emblazoned across the front. Charlie, along with most everyone else in this area, was a Washington Redskins fan, but it didn't matter. Jay had other things going for him. Not only had he learned in the Agency about bugging rooms, cars and other stationary and moving things, he had also learned how to enter locked and secure buildings, how to blow up structures, cars and other things and how to use a wide variety of weapons and tools of harm and destruction—including his two hands. He was known as one tough and efficient operator.

"I'm not sure I give a rat's ass what you believe, Henderson," Buckner said. "But think about it for a minute. First, try to come up with a reason I would have for knowing. Then come up with one for my knowing and not telling you."

Charlie did as he was told; he thought about it for a minute. Then he said, "OK, you have my apologies."

"Accepted."

"Will you find out for me?"

"Why?"

"I have a hunch it might help."

"Help what?"

"Josh."

"Josh surely knows what's going on there. Ask him."

"I did but he wouldn't tell me."

"I don't get it, but what about Sam or Gene or one of the others? One of them is bound to know."

"I think Scotty knew. But I don't want to ask the others. I just want to find out. Will you do it?"

They were approaching the right turn off to Middleway, a tiny historic community. They were only five or so minutes now from Hillmont.

"You're talking a late-night bag job, aren't you?"

"How you do it is up to you."

Jay dimmed the lights for an approaching car. "I've never burglarized an Agency building before . . ."

"Look, I am not asking you to do that. Security must be terrific around the place."

"I understand security is now tight as twins because of Ames. The soft Charmin days are over—for a while, at least."

"Be careful, Jay. Your getting caught would not be good for you or for any of us."

"The Russians and the Iranians and the French and the Argentines and all the others never caught me doing anything. I'm not going to get caught now."

And then, in that last minute as they drove down the gravel road to Hillmont, Jay Buckner, never a close friend anyhow, pricked Charlie's rawest vulnerability.

"You shouldn't feel guilty about what happened to Scotty," Buckner said. "You really shouldn't."

"I don't," Charlie said. "I really don't."

"Good. If it hadn't been your thing with the Senate it would have been something else. He was clearly sick."

Charlie thanked Jay for the ride and got out of the car.

I did not kill Scotty.

He really did not feel any serious guilt about Scotty. In fact, he believed he had made it possible for Scotty to die on the job—a kind of "in the line of duty" death.

PART 2

MARTY

October

FIVE

Marty Madigan had already decided that when he became a U.S. senator he would be one of a new kind. He would do the job with a unique seriousness that would set him apart from all other senators, including all who had come before. He would establish himself as an independent mind and voice for the broadest national interest. He would reject all appeals from all narrow special interests, including appeals from special interests in his own state. He would accept no campaign contributions except from himself and members of his family. He would speak only on national and international issues and only to serious nonpolitical groups such as world affairs councils, think tanks and university seminars. He would seldom make trips home to campaign, on grounds that he was a full-time senator not a politician. He would entertain no constituent groups in his Washington office and would provide no constituent services to the people back home. His staff would be made up entirely of experts with advanced degrees in fields related to major issues and concerns. His time at the office would be spent in quiet study and contemplation or in vigorous discussion with his brilliant staff and others as he sought truth, challenge and guidance through the process of intellectual exercise and give-and-take. He would not take or read polls, refusing to know or care what his constituents might think about any issue. They had elected him to be his own man and that he would always be.

Meanwhile, however, he would have to do the kind of thing he was doing right now, which was running alongside Senator Lank Simmons, Republican, of New Mexico, in a hallway of the U.S. Capitol.

"Johnny Field at the NSC just called," Marty said to Simmons. "He confirmed that Bennett is the president's choice."

"For what?"

"For director of Central Intelligence. He's the DDCI now . . ."

"Jesus, yes, Marty. I'm sorry. Much on the plate this morning. They're trying to take away our water." He turned to another man, running along on his other side. "Where is that water-table file from the Corps of Engineers?"

"There in your right hand, sir," said the aide.

"Sure, sure. Sorry." Simmons turned back to Marty Madigan.

"The White House wants to know the senator's reaction to Bennett," Marty said.

"What *is* our reaction, Marty?"

"We haven't had a chance to talk it through yet, Senator."

"Right, right. Ride with me to the Ritz-Carlton in thirty minutes. I've got a wave-through to do at a luncheon. And bring the clips. I haven't had time to go through the clips yet this morning."

"Yes, sir," said Marty. The clips were cuttings from various newspapers, including all twenty of New Mexico's dailies, of stories about people, issues and events that were thought to be of particular interest to the senator.

The senator and the water aide disappeared on down the hall.

And Marty, as he watched them go, returned briefly to thoughts about himself.

He would never ask a staff member what he should think about anything. He would arrive at his positions on his own after carefully weighing the pros and cons. He would decide on whether to support a presidential nominee only after personally reviewing the nominee's qualifications and background, after giving the position as well as the person intense scrutiny. He would never allow partisan politics to become a factor . . .

Marty had made the decision to be a United States senator in 1974 when he was twelve years old. Watergate was the reason. That year, Marty watched every minute of the Senate

Watergate hearings on television—if not live, then the public television repeats at night. He did so originally because he had to as middle-school history homework. But he came to see the hearings as a great adventure and the senators as heroic gladiators—honest, fearless, dedicated, nonpolitical men pursuing the truth about an evil president. It was made even more real to Marty because one of the committee members was Senator Lowell Weicker, a Republican from Marty's own state of Connecticut. Marty's father was a leading Weicker supporter in their town and Marty had met him a few times.

Someday, thought Marty, then and now, he would be a Weicker—or a Sam Ervin or a Howard Baker, his principal Watergate heroes—doing heroic work as a United States senator for the American people.

But, for now, he moved at half-trot on down the hallway to arrange for a senator named Simmons to get the clips and an opinion about a nominee for director of Central Intelligence.

As the second-ranking Republican leader of the Senate, Lank Simmons was entitled to a chauffeur-driven car. But not only could he not use that car, he had to make a big thing of not using it. That was because he first got elected by defeating a Democratic incumbent partly on a get-the-bureaucrats-out-of-those-limousines campaign line. Then, to show off the idea that he was a serious person, the very first thing he did as a freshman senator was introduce some show-off legislation that would have prevented all government officials below the president and vice president from having government limos. Simmons got the national television time and newspaper ink he wanted for the grandstand effort, but now and forever he was stuck. No more limos for him, now and forever.

So that was why Marty was sitting in the front passenger seat while Simmons drove his own five-year-old Ford station wagon down Pennsylvania Avenue toward the Ritz-Carlton.

Marty was talking: "Bennett's a professional with nothing on the books that would seem to disqualify him. He's had experience on both the covert and overt sides. He's never got himself caught in a high-visibility crack of any kind. His fingerprints are nowhere on the Ames case. He was in another part of the world and of the Agency and thus way out of the loop on Iran-Contra. He was a brand-new agent during Watergate. He is as far I can tell completely nonpartisan and nonpolitical. I see no reason why we shouldn't give him a thumbs-up."

"What does Bushong think?"

"I haven't asked."

"Ask, just so we can say we did. He's ours, remember."

"Yes, sir."

"Anything in the clips about Bennett to worry about?"

"No, sir. Only a few stories, all either neutral or positive."

"Anything else about anything else in the clips?"

"Nothing to mention."

Simmons said, "The Faucet made some noise about Bennett just now. What's that all about?"

That didn't make sense to Marty. "He's not on our committee and he's not armed services or foreign relations either."

Hank Grover was the Faucet. He was the harshly partisan senior Democratic senator from Texas who chaired the Water Resources Subcommittee of the Senate Commerce Committee, whose meeting Simmons had just attended. His absolute power over water policy in the United States had earned him his nickname. Cross him, he turns off your water and your state becomes a desert overnight.

"Well, he's got something up something about Bennett," Simmons said.

"What exactly did he say?"

Simmons was maneuvering the car into the narrow circular driveway in front of the Ritz-Carlton. "'I hope you intelligence people have the intelligence to keep that Bennett nomination from happening.' That's what he said. Something like that. Why don't you come in with me?"

"No, thanks, Senator. I'll just hang out in the lobby or somewhere . . ."

"Come on, Marty. It'll be good training for a young man of the future."

Marty had been to many wave-throughs as well as walk-throughs and smile-throughs and shout-throughs and talk-throughs and the other demeaning events required of United States senators and all others seeking or holding public office. And he was about to go to another right now. He had no choice.

Marty had no idea what the luncheon or the people attending it were all about. There were a hundred and fifty or so of them at round tables for ten in half of the hotel's main ballroom. When Simmons, with Marty two paces back, walked through the door, two men rushed to them.

"Senator, Senator . . . terrific that you came," said one of them. "Great to see you, Senator, great to see you," said the other.

One of them gestured to a man at a table up front. He leaped to his feet and to a microphone behind a podium on a small stage. A red-white-and-blue banner on the podium proclaimed "The Washington Future" but proclaimed nothing more. What Washington future, and for whom?

"Ladies and gentlemen, if I could have your attention please." The room was small enough, the audience savvy enough and Lank Simmons tall and recognizable enough for everyone to know what was about to happen. They quickly got quiet.

"We have a surprise visitor," said the man at the microphone. "He has just come from an important hearing and can literally only give us a smile and a wave. But we are honored for that. I give you the assistant minority leader of the United States Senate, the tall man from New Mexico, Lank Simmons!"

All of the people stood and applauded and Simmons waved at them. Quickly and deliberately he moved from table to table, steadily approaching the podium.

"It's hard to keep a politician away from a live microphone," he said to the group. "I just wanted to say a formal hello, a formal welcome to Washington, a formal yes to the question 'Is there anyone in Washington who knows what needs to be done and is doing it?' "

The audience loved that and showed their love with deeper laughs and claps.

"And what I must do now is go do what I know must be done. Thank you and good luck in all that you undertake for yourselves, your loved ones and your America."

Marty, who had remained at the back of the ballroom, recognized that last sentence. Everyone who had heard Simmons speak more than once would have, because that was the way he ended every public appearance.

Twelve minutes after they had left the car with the doorman, Simmons and Marty were back out on Massachusetts Avenue headed back to the Capitol.

"I hate those things," Simmons mumbled to Marty.

"Why do them then? You're the assistant minority leader of the United States Senate. You don't have to do that kind of thing anymore."

"Yes, I do, Marty, if I want to remain the assistant minority leader of the United States Senate."

"Who were they anyhow?"

Lank Simmons tossed his head about, smiled and said, "College presidents, I think. Right. Some kind of higher-education group. It's there on that card."

Somebody in Lank Simmons's office had typed up his day's schedule on a stack of small index cards. Marty picked up the card on top. The entry for the event they had just attended was "Annual meeting, Presidents and Past Presidents of the American Pharmaceutical Association."

"You'll touch the bases for me on Bennett, right?" Simmons said to Marty before they parted in the Senate garage.

"I will," Marty replied.

"The Faucet and Bushong?"

"Yes, sir."

Marty was no fan of Russell Bushong, who was known by all as a man dedicated to his own interests. But in the words of Senator Simmons, Bushong was "ours"—meaning his interests often coincided with those of the minority members and staff of the Senate Intelligence Committee.

Marty's afternoon rendezvous with Bushong was set for four thirty-five at the Mall entrance to the Smithsonian's National Museum of American History. Marty was there on time and two minutes later Bushong drove up in his mahogany-brown XJ6 Jaguar. He stopped it right there at the curb, got out, locked the door and walked toward Marty.

Marty, as always, was struck by Bushong's props. That brown car and his aviator-rim sunglasses and his tweed coat and blue button-down Oxford-cloth shirt—they were all props for a senior intelligence officer, a role Bushong played well.

"You can't just leave that car there like that, Russ," Marty said immediately. "That is the ultimate killer tow-away zone. You'll never see that beautiful Jag of yours again. It'll never survive that city towed-car lot under the Whitehurst Freeway in Georgetown . . ."

"No problem," said Bushong coolly, as if he were waving off a light sprinkle of rain.

The car was indeed beautiful there in the autumn sunshine. It was absolutely spotless and the sun made its finish sparkle like a precious stone.

"I'm serious," Marty said, as they began walking together. "They have the fastest tow trucks in America on this mall."

Bushong, as if communicating nuclear secrets, whispered, "I can park anywhere, anytime. I'm tow-truck-proof."

Automatically, Marty responded in an equally hushed tone. "How in the hell is the Smithsonian or Park Police cop who comes by here going to know . . ."

"I promise you, Marty, that my car will be here, untowed, unharmed and fully accounted for, when we return."

And they walked on into the museum.

"I assume there will someday be the dress of your first lady here, Marty?" Bushong said as the two of them walked along, together with mobs of schoolkids and other visitors, in front of the First Ladies' Inaugural Gown display.

Oh, Bushong, you smart devil, you, thought Marty. In a senatorial voice, he said, "The gentleman assumes correctly."

It had been Bushong's suggestion that they meet on the Mall in front of the history museum. He always suggested rendezvous spots like that as a way of helping his lay co-convenor think he was doing something secret and exciting. It was not unlike the fantasy experiences that the Dodgers and other major league baseball teams provide for men who pay to come to play baseball in mock two-week training camps with retired major league ballplayers.

"First the Senate, of course?" said Bushong. "No county commissioner's or House seat first, of course?"

"Of course."

"You would run from Connecticut, I assume?"

"Again, the gentleman assumes correctly."

Two happy, smiling men of Washington talking the routine small talk of their city.

Bushong said, "I may have something for you on Devers when the time comes."

"That would be most helpful, Russ. Thanks."

Devers was Reggie Devers, the current Republican junior senator from Connecticut, who was a member of the Senate Intelligence Committee and a good friend of Marty's and Simmons's. But one does have to plan for all contingencies, for all emergencies, thought Marty. What bastards we are, you and me, Bushong.

Time now for their real Washington business. "Josh Bennett is why I called," Marty said to Bushong. "The White House wants a quick reading from Simmons. Simmons wants a quick reading from you."

Bushong was way ahead of him. "I anticipated such a request and I have come prepared for such a reading." He beamed.

What a *smart* bastard you are, Russ Bushong. And don't you know it.

Bushong handed Marty an unmarked manila envelope. Marty took it. It felt thick.

"As always," said Bushong, in the exaggerated tone of a movie spy chief, "nothing in this can ever be attributed to me. Anyone who violates that edict will face dire consequences and recriminations in this life and all that might follow."

"I tremble at the thought of such recriminations, sir." Marty knew the game.

Bushong stopped walking. They were now approaching

the transportation section of the museum, where there was a huge, marvelous, fully restored Southern Railway steam locomotive. Marty could hear the *shshshshshshshshsh* sound of the recording that was played for the tourists to give the scene a feel of realism.

"Don't make light of me, young man, and what I do for you, for the United States Senate and the people of the United States," said Bushong, suddenly quite serious. "There are hundreds of intelligence officers out there every moment of every day putting their lives and minds on the line for their country and their beliefs. We are a silent, secret force for democracy, freedom and right. Never make light of us or our work. Never put us down. Never attack us with a smile or smirk. Ames hurt us and embarrassed us but he did not destroy us."

"I meant no offense," Marty said. "I thought you were playing a bit yourself . . ."

Now Marty was truly confused. Was Bushong putting him on with that earlier crap about consequences or what? Confusion, Marty's predecessor had advised him, was one of the principal tools used by the people from Langley. They get nervous with outsiders who seem to understand them or what they're really doing.

"Do you like trains, Marty?"

"Yeah, kind of."

"I thought so. You seemed like a trains man. I would have preferred we meet at the National Gallery. The Nasher sculpture collection is back in the East Wing. Are you into sculpture as well as trains?"

"I've been to the Nasher exhibition seven times already. I have never seen a better collection of Moores and Giacomettis."

"Next time we'll do sculpture."

It wasn't long before they were back outside. The Jag was still there, untowed and unharmed and glistening, in a killer tow-away zone.

"There she is," said Bushong. "The most exquisite motor vehicle ever designed and built. There she is. The Jaguar XJ6, the ultimate artifact of our civilization that we will leave for the anthropologists and archeologists and tour directors of the future to unearth and study and admire. It is as much a piece of art as anything in the Nasher collection. Look at her, Marty. Look with admiration and envy."

"I don't get it," Marty said. "Please, explain to me why this artifact of our civilization was not towed away."

"Do you promise silence?"

"So promised."

"All right, come around then to the rear license plate," said Bushong, lowering his voice to a pretend conspiratorial tone.

They walked to the back of the car. Bushong leaned down to the plate and Marty leaned down with him. "See this?" Bushong said, pointing to a circle in the lower-left-hand corner of the plate, which appeared to Marty to be a standard Virginia license. The circle was slightly smaller than a dime and was a bright purple.

Still whispering, Bushong said, "This little dot is something relatively new—something I am proud to say that I have been working on for years. All police officers in all jurisdictions in the Washington area are instructed to check for this button-sized dot on all license plates before calling for a tow truck—or taking any other direct action against an illegally parked vehicle. If they see this purple dot they are to radio or call for further instructions."

"What are these things made of?" Marty asked.

"A material that our labs developed that is special and impossible to duplicate."

"How many people have a purple dot?"

"All of us who matter," Bushong said.

"Can you get me one?"

"Kill the Bennett nomination and I'll see what I can do."

Marty had taken a taxi from his office on the Hill down to the Mall and the Smithsonian. But why not walk back? He figured he could do it in twenty-five minutes; it was a beautiful afternoon and the exercise would be good for him.

He didn't get far. The weight of his curiosity about what was in Bushong's envelope slowed him down and eventually stopped him at a bench just beyond the National Gallery's East Wing.

The first page was an unsigned, unheaded and undated double-spaced typed memorandum. It said:

"Joshua Bennett would be a disaster as DCI. Documentary evidence concerning some of the most serious areas of concern is attached. Most of it provides leads for further inquiry. Information on the other charges can be obtained through the taking of testimony from present and past employees of his organization."

Marty turned to the first page of the documentary evidence.

It was the internal report on what happened with the Czech, Charles Henderson and Joshua Bennett in West Berlin. There were more than forty pages of interviews and investigative notes and observations. On the last page somebody—Marty assumed it was Bushong—had used a red marker pencil to circle the following comment:

"We are of the opinion that the failure of this operation was avoidable. There is no evidence that (name deleted) and/or (name deleted) did anything that would indicate any intentional desire to have it end in failure. But it is clear that one or both made a mistake in judgment. Unfortunately, we were not able to determine with certainty either the substance or even the nature of the mistake or exactly which of the two made it."

Just outside the red circle was the final sentence: "We recommend that no disciplinary action be taken."

The next group of papers—thirty-seven pages in all—were copies of expense vouchers for hotels, meals, rental cars and other travel activities in a wide variety of countries all over the world. The name of the person filing them was deleted.

Marty thumbed through them. They meant nothing to him and he doubted if they would to anyone else. If this was documentary evidence that Josh Bennett would be a disaster as DCI, he did not see it.

So much for killing the Bennett nomination, so much for getting a purple dot for his BMW 325i.

He debated ducking into the National Gallery, right behind him, for an eighth look at Jonathan Borofsky's twenty-foot-high *Hammering Man* sculpture in the Patsy and Raymond Nasher Collection. But no. There was more to be done for America before he played or rested this day.

The most important thing to be done was to spend some time with Andrea Bartlett, the most beautiful liberal he had ever known.

It didn't have to be Andrea Bartlett. Marty had several other routes he could have traveled in trying to find out what Senator Grover, the Faucet, had working against Josh Bennett— and why. Most involved talking to men on various staffs who were close to the staffs of Grover or one of the committees or subcommittees he ruled with an iron—faucet. Going the Andrea route bordered on being an act of masochism. She was the general counsel of the Senate Commerce Committee, parent to Grover's water subcommittee, in addition to being a smart, gorgeous liberal.

At first she did what she usually did. She refused to see him. "Forget it, Marty," she said when he called to ask her to dinner. "We are not politically or philosophically or any other way compatible. I am busy, you are busy. Let's just smile in the hall and across conference tables and let it go at that."

He persisted and triumphed with an I-swear-on-the-

Constitution-of-the-United-States-and-the-Republican-Party-Platform promise that it was strictly business. Strictly urgent national security business.

Marty used Senator Simmons's name in reserving a quiet corner table at Sfuzzi, a smart and noisy Italian bar and restaurant in the remarkably rehabilitated and revived Union Station building, the new mecca of smart shops, theaters and restaurants for Capitol Hill workers and residents as well as train travelers.

"This is ridiculous, really dumb, Marty," she said once they were seated. "I have to be at a meeting back in the office at nine."

"Shut up and enjoy yourself while you're here," Marty said.

Shut up? He just told Andrea Bartlett to shut up!

"I'm sorry I told you to shut up," he said, feeling a blast of furnace red in his face. "It just popped out."

"You were right to say it," she said. "What's the urgent business?"

"Would you please at least look at the menu first?"

"Shut up and order, is that it?" She opened the thick leather-bound menu in front of her.

Marty had to look at his menu, too, although he would have much preferred simply watching her look at hers with those magnificent blue eyes in that perfectly proportioned creamy-olive-complexioned face surrounded by perfectly cut and groomed dark brown hair.

Within minutes a waiter had taken her order, spinach ravioli, and his, thin-crust cheeseless vegetable pizza. Both ordered a mozzarella-and-tomato salad to start and he chose a thirty-two-dollar bottle of Chianti to go with it all.

"I'm only going to have a tiny sip," she said. "Don't spend a fortune on this."

"There's no better way to spend a fortune than on a good bottle of wine, Ms. Bartlett," he said.

"Spoken like a real Republican."

"Responded to like a real Democrat."

The wine was delivered and Marty took his time smelling the cork and sipping and sucking before pronouncing the Chianti drinkable and pourable.

Then, once both glasses were filled, he raised his to Andrea and she responded in kind. "To you, the single best asset the Democrats have on Capitol Hill," he said.

"I think what you just said was sexist," she said.

"Exceedingly so," he replied.

Their salads were put on the table. And after taking a first bite of mozzarella, Marty said, "Do you have a purple dot on your license plate?"

"I not only do not have one, I have never heard of such a thing," she said. "I truly hope and pray that purple dots on license plates are not the urgent national security matters you had on your mind for tonight." She stuffed salad into her mouth as fast as it would conveniently go.

All right, Marty thought. There will be no small talk, there will be no nothing except business and she will be out of here. So be it.

"I want to know what the Faucet has against Josh Bennett at CIA."

"I have no idea."

"Come on now, Andrea. Grover's hates and wishes are well known by every subject in his kingdom."

"I'm not a part of his kingdom."

"You know everyone who is."

He noticed with delight that she had already had three of those tiny sips of his Republican wine. A superior woman cannot resist a superior wine—even if she can resist the superior man that goes with it.

"Why doesn't Simmons just ask Grover?" Andrea said. "Even in Washington it is sometimes possible to do things directly—to just come right out with it."

"Simmons, for some reason, doesn't want to do it that way."

"It probably hasn't occurred to him, that's why. Is he really as stupid and smarmy as he appears to be?"

"Are any of them?" No, in fact, they're not, he thought. And fervently believed most of the time.

"It is Washington's great secret," she said. "United States senators, like many others here, are not really as stupid and smarmy as they appear to be."

"Hear ye, hear ye, we have news from Washington!"

"Do you see a Senator Madigan in your future?" she asked.

"Yes, as a matter of fact. Do you see a Senator Bartlett?"

"Maybe so."

And in a few minutes the main courses were served. The high-water mark was now about halfway down the wine bottle.

It turned out that Andrea had once wanted to be a sculptor and had been three times to see the Nasher Collection—once when it was at the National Gallery the first time, a few years ago.

It turned out that Andrea and Marty shared a desire, born of college classics courses, to sail the Aegean Sea sometime, exploring and experiencing the ancient ruins of Epidaurus, Delphi, Ephesus and Troy.

It turned out that both never traveled without a spy novel in their briefcases, the result of a lifelong love of good espionage and detective stories. Marty said le Carré was the best. Andrea was more partial to Charles McCarry.

It turned out that just before nine o'clock Andrea decided the meeting in her office could be handled by the associate counsel and she took a cellular telephone out of her purse and notified all concerned of that fact.

It turned out that when they said good night at Andrea's car in the Senate garage it was almost eleven-fifteen and she said she would see what she could find out about Grover and Bennett. She said she would try to get back to Marty sometime the next day.

There were five messages on his answering machine from Jane Culver, Senator Simmons's appointments person. She was a self-important women of forty or so who had come to Washington with Simmons as his secretary sixteen years ago. They were the worst kind, these I-was-there-when-He-was-nothing people, called lifers or believers by others on the Hill.

They believed their presence at the birth gave them inalienable rights and power over all others. But with all of that, Marty liked Jane. She had a sense of humor and she was smart as hell.

The pitch and volume of her voice on the machine rose with each message. The last one was delivered at close to a full shriek.

"Marty. This is Jane again. Goddamn it, it is urgent that Himself talk to you. Where are you? Why didn't you take your beeper? Get a phone or a fax or something for that fancy car of yours. If it's before ten-twenty now when you are listening to this, call Himself at home. If it's not, don't. He's going to bed at ten-twenty. Either way, meet him in the morning at five forty-five at the Georgetown University track. He would prefer you jog, too, so you two can talk. Either way, be there. He'll ask about the clips as usual. Tell him they're in the works as usual. He has two prayer breakfasts and three morning walk-throughs so the jog will end at six thirty-five or so at the latest. Sleep well. Seriously, Marty, you should remember that you are involved in intelligence work. You should never be unreachable. I'm serious. The Russians might rise again. Or Castro might need killing—again. Sleep well. Good night. Assuming you got home. You didn't spend the whole night out, did you? Too much sex dulls the male mind. You have just got to tell us where you are and what you are doing. What if Ollie North needs help selling arms to somebody? Sleep well."

I was at the train station falling in love, Jane.

As he drove home in his white BMW 325i he had looked

into the rearview mirror, caught his reflection in the windshield and seen Spencer Tracy both times. Tracy and Hepburn, Madigan and Bartlett. Spence and Kate, Marty and Andrea.

Love overcomes all and everything?

Home was a deluxe condo in Georgetown. It was in a place south of M Street on the C&O Canal called the Tannery, which supposedly it really had been before a developer converted it into living and office spaces. The best thing about it was location. A Habitat store, where he bought most of his furniture and related things, was at the end of his street. Dean & Deluca was just across a footbridge for exotic food and drink, as was Georgetown Park, a three-level shopping mall with a Victorian motif and shops that sold most everything he would ever want.

Jog with Simmons at five forty-five in the morning? OK. Tell him the clips are in the works.

Sleep well? You bet.

SIX

Marty had always been an enthusiastic and conscientious runner. He enjoyed the steady moving of his body for what it did to keep him in shape physically and also for the uplift it gave his spirit. A sense of well-being often came upon him while running that brought tears to his eyes.

But there was none of that when he ran alongside Senator Simmons. They might as well have been walking down a hallway at the Capitol or sitting in a hearing room or office. It was all business.

"We no longer have a choice, Marty," said the senator

within seconds after they had taken their first extended stride together.

"Nothing has turned up on Bennett," Marty replied. "Not one thing."

"Find something."

"You can't find what's not there, sir."

"What did Bushong say?" The senator was in as terrific physical shape as Marty was. Not even his voice gave a sign that he was talking while moving at a steady lope.

"Lots, but it's mostly crap." Marty, at six feet even, was more than five inches shorter than Lank Simmons, but fortunately his legs were long. He could match the senator's long stride without too much difficulty.

After several seconds of silence, Simmons said, "Talk to him again, turn his crap into crepe. Whatever. Get me the stuff to kill the nomination."

They finished their first turn around the quarter-mile track. "I am not sure that's possible," said Marty.

"Politics is nothing if not the art and craft of the impossible."

Marty, still in sync with the senator's gait, let that piece of wisdom get lost in the sound of their running shoes pounding against the cinder track.

Then he said, "Why do we have to do this, Senator?"

"So the people of eastern New Mexico can have water."

"That's it?"

"That's it. I got it right from the Faucet's own spout last night. Where were you last night, by the way? We looked everywhere."

Marty felt sweat for the first time. It was on his forehead and down his back. He chose to ignore the question and ask one of his own. "Did the Faucet tell you why?"

"No, and I didn't ask. All I care about is that water. Josh Bennett doesn't live or vote in New Mexico."

"I'm not sure I can do this . . ."

"Two prayer breakfasts and three walk-throughs, all before nine, is what I am doing this morning for America, Marty. The least you can do is find the information to stop the Bennett nomination."

"Senator, this isn't right . . ."

They made another lap and a half in silence before the senator said, "Where are the clips, Marty?"

"They're in the works, Senator." Marty was delighted to see perspiration forming around Simmons's eyes.

"I like to have the clips the first thing in the morning from the first staff person I talk to."

Marty already knew that, of course. It was part of the gospel that governed the office and staff of Senator Simmons.

And soon they had been around the track eight times. The jog was over.

As Marty slowed down to a walk, the Republican whip of the Senate said, "See you in the office, Marty," and he broke into a sprint.

The senator was through the gate and out of sight before Marty could reply.

Marty kept walking by himself. He needed some cool-down time. The track was the one the Georgetown University track team used. It was marked out by whitewash lines into six running lanes. There was a grass football field in the center and several rows of bleachers on either side, left over, he guessed, from the days when Georgetown fielded a football team.

He made another full lap around the track. Coming back north he paid attention for the first time to the various buildings of the Georgetown University Hospital ahead, just outside the fence. He had been in the hospital several times to visit friends and colleagues and had looked this way out their windows.

There were people at a few of the windows now, looking down on him and the dozen or so other early-morning joggers. Most of the people in the windows appeared to be dressed in pajamas and robes. He waved and most waved back.

At least he wasn't one of them, he thought. At least he hadn't had a heart attack or been shot in a holdup or had a tumor removed from his brain.

His only ailment was in his soul. And no amount of jogging was going to make it go away.

They stood at the railing on the mezzanine floor. Off and down to the right was the *Hammering Man*. Marty, for reasons he could never explain, really connected with sculpture. It had the same nutritious effect on him as running.

There was something transporting, transforming, about watching this huge black-metal moving figure of a man hammering. Directly ahead, suspended from the sky-high ceiling, was a giant red, black and blue mobile by Alexander Calder. On the first floor on the left was George Segal's fabulous *Rush Hour,* seven life-sized, realistic people in bronze, waiting for a bus or the light to change or something. Directly behind them on the mezzanine were several Giacomettis and Claes Oldenberg's strange *Pile of Typewriter Erasers,* which was nothing more—or less—than a pile of larger-than-life typewriter erasers.

"I am about to give you a piece of paper," Bushong said. "Two names with addresses are on it."

Marty took the paper, which was white and slightly larger than an index card.

"That first one is the man who was principal of the high school in Massachusetts from which our subject graduated. He has an interesting story to tell if you can get him to tell it."

Marty read the typed name and address: Richard Crystal Winslow, 526 South Ash, Westwood, Massachusetts.

"The second one is a close friend and former associate of our subject. He is now retired and runs an overpriced bed-and-breakfast out in the West Virginia Panhandle. He, too, has a story to tell that he has never told, primarily, I think, because of his close friendship with Bennett. He just sent him a Jesus hat, in fact. That's how close they are."

"Jesus hat?"

"Never mind. They were teamed together a lot, including that West Berlin fiasco. That's the story you want from him. He was the one who got the Blue Heart out of it."

"Blue Heart?"

"It's what we call the certificates we give people when

they're wounded or hurt. 'Blue Heart' as in 'Purple Heart.' Our little conceit."

Marty read the second typed name and address: Charles Avenue Henderson, Hillmont, Rural Route 2, Charles Town, West Virginia.

"They named the town for him?" Marty said.

"The town was named for Charles Washington, one of George's brothers."

"Avenue?"

"Charlie claims his mother named him that because she was born on a Charles Avenue in some Missouri town . . . Sedalia, Columbia, one of those."

"You obviously know this guy."

"I know him well. He was sometimes very good at what he did for us."

"What was it that he did?"

"He was what we call a warrior."

"Warrior as in Comanche?"

"Warrior as in watch your scalp and your ass if you decide to fool with him. There is nothing in our little bag of tricks—dirty or clean—that Henderson wasn't a part of for nearly forty years. Covert, overt, soft, hard, here, there, everywhere."

"He must be an old man now."

"His kind don't age like the rest of us, Marty."

Forty-five minutes later Marty was still standing at the mezzanine railing looking down at the *Hammering Man* and other attractions of the Nasher Collection. Beside him now stood Andrea Bartlett. Marty had arranged a doubleheader at the National Gallery's East Wing.

"I studied it and I even did some of it but I still don't fully understand it," she said to Marty. They were speaking about the power and pull of sculpture.

"Maybe the cliché about trying to understand art is true," he said.

She said nothing. He waited a few seconds and said, "You know the one I mean?"

"Certainly. But it's not a cliché, it's a truism."

Marty prided himself on being a fairly accurate reader of body language. And he did not like what he was picking up from this beautiful body next to him. For whatever reason, Andrea Bartlett clearly wished she was not here. Could it be that she really does detest me as a person? This was an alien thought to Marty. He had been loved and admired by most everyone he had met in his life, from the hospital delivery room in Westport, Connecticut, onward. He had enjoyed the appreciation of nearly every female he had encountered since the fifth grade. None had ever turned him down or away. The result had been years of pleasant, intense relationships with smart, attractive women that ended, each in its own way, mostly because his passion for job and future ran roughshod over all other passions.

At his suggestion, they moved to a position in front of Matisse's voluptuous bronze *Large Seated Nude.*

"No problem understanding this one, I bet," he said.

She gave Marty a look that screamed, Shut up!

And she told him what she had come to tell him.

"There is no real policy reason. Grover's apparently setting up a swap of some kind."

"A swap?"

"He's got a friend from Texas—an old lawyer friend—whom he wants appointed to the Fifth Circuit Court of Appeals. The White House has already promised the job to somebody else. I was told by someone—third-hand, I must tell you—that Grover may want to use Simmons to put a vise on the Bennett nomination and then make a trade for the judgeship."

"'You give me the judge, I give you Bennett'?"

"That's it."

"That's outrageous!"

"That's the United States Senate. You know that as well as I do so please spare me your 'shocked' routine. And keep your voice down. This is a museum."

Marty looked around to see if anyone was staring at him. Nobody was. But Andrea was right. To play shocked and shout over this kind of Senate swap smacked of hypocrisy—at least in the world of the U.S. Senate as it was today. He hoped someday to change all that.

A few minutes later they were sitting at a table in the restaurant in the passageway between the East Wing and the main building.

"I have to decide what to do," he said. "I'm not sure I want to be a party to such a weird and unfair game. He'll probably still end up being DCI, but Josh Bennett doesn't deserve to be put through such a thing . . ."

Andrea shook her head violently. "No more. Not another word about this." Marty had a feeling she would have clubbed him silent if he had not stopped talking.

She continued: "What I just told you is as far as I go. I don't want ever again to be a source of information for some right-wing Republican senator—*your* right-wing Republican senator—who has stood in the way of most that is progressive and good for this country."

Marty reached across the table and took her right hand in his. It felt as cold as the glass of iced tea he was drinking. "Fine, no problem," he said. "I appreciate what you have done . . ."

And her cold hand slipped away from his warm one.

They went back to discussing the mysterious power of sculpture—how a British sculptor named Long could lay out five pieces of gray Welsh slate on the floor and make it art.

And then as lunch was about to end, he gathered his courage and said:

"I hereby invite you to go to a high-class bed-and-breakfast in West Virginia for the weekend." He told her about a *Baltimore Sun* article about the place that he pulled off the Internet. It said it was a great combination of history and elegance.

She was already gathering her purse to leave. At first he wasn't sure she had even heard him. Finally she said, "I have a meeting Saturday night."

"A business meeting?"

"Yes."

"Do you go on regular dates?"

"Yes. Usually with a man I have gone out with off and on for years."

"Good."

"Good?"

"That you have been going out for years."

"That's a stupid thing to say."

Oh, how right you are, Marty thought. I've been so busy preparing for my glorious future that I have forgotten how to court. No, he thought again. Maybe the problem is that I never really had to learn.

Marty was at a pay phone near the museum restaurant within moments after Andrea left. He said all of the proper things ("It's a matter of national security") to Jane Culver, who reluctantly patched the call through to the senator. "He's on the mobile phone—the tiny one—and he's moving fast down the halls of the Hart Building so you better make it quick," she said to Marty. "Timber in west New Mexico is at stake in that hearing."

There was a crackling and a modest beep on the line with Simmons's voice. But the senator said he could hear fine.

"Are you alone enough, Senator?"

"Nobody around here is ever alone enough, Marty."

"Should I tell you what I just learned about motives and the Faucet and Bennett?"

"Shoot, please. By all means, shoot."

Marty told him about the water, the judgeship, the White House and all the rest.

"That is truly great news, Marty," said the senator, or at least that was what it sounded like to Marty. "Congratulations."

Marty couldn't believe it. Congratulations? What in the hell is the man saying?

"Sir, it's all a smokescreen to get a Texas friend appointed to the federal bench," Marty repeated. "It's a sham—"

"I know, that's terrific. Good work."

"Senator, please. What Grover is doing is a goddamn outrage. We can't be a party to this—"

"I'm at the hearing room, got to run. The timber boys are depending on me. Everyone wants to settle the West, Marty. That's the problem. They won't leave us alone. They want to come tell us how to grow our trees and cut our trees just like they want to tell us how to use our water and treat our Indians. It's our timber and our water, Marty, and the Indians are our people. None of them, none of it belongs to Washington and the president and the Senate. It's ours and I am going to make sure it stays ours. Everything that is ours stays ours, Marty. They are not going to destroy our way of life with their federal rules and regulations and guidelines and fees. The people of New Mexico elected me to protect them from all of this and that is what I am doing. And that is all I am doing. Now get me some good stuff on Bennett so I can keep our end of the bargain with the Faucet so we can keep our water."

"I'm having trouble understanding you."

"We have to have the goods on Bennett just like it's for real. Otherwise it won't work. Happy hunting. Have you seen the story in the clips about IBM looking for a place to build a new chips plant?"

"I saw it, yes, sir."

"Let's get on it, Marty. We've got lots of perfect places in New Mexico for new IBM plants."

"I'm only your intelligence man, Senator—"

"Right, right. Sorry."

The phone went dead in Marty's ear.

He walked back into the East Wing. He stood at the base of the *Hammering Man* and looked twenty feet up as the right arm came down and went back up as if in a slow-motion movie.

Simmons was right, of course, about one thing—the big thing. The threat to kill the Bennett nomination for Grover had to have teeth to it or the White House would never buckle and appoint the El Paso lawyer . . .

He returned to the pay phone. A woman with a quiet, pleasant voice hesitated before taking his reservation for the weekend. She said he was truly in luck because it wasn't five minutes ago that they had had a cancellation. Usually, she said, calls this late could not be accommodated.

He didn't believe a word of what she said but it made perfect sense that a bed-and-breakfast owned and operated by a former CIA warrior would put out cover stories.

Marty had no idea what to expect at this West Virginia place called Hillmont, from this warrior named Henderson. He had gone to his apartment, grabbed his tuxedo and a few other clothes that he felt would be appropriate for an eighteenth-century weekend in the country. Do I need an Uzi, too? What about a poison detector and a room debugger?

The woman on the phone had said there were two routes to Hillmont—a pretty one that included some two-lane highway and a not-so-pretty one that was all interstate and freeway. Depending on the traffic both took around an hour and a half, she said. He chose the pretty one.

Marty had lived in and around Washington for more than ten years but he had never come up this far west and north. His only awareness of the area had to do with Harpers Ferry, where John Brown was caught and where Thomas Jefferson stood on a rock and marveled at a view.

He drove past Dulles Airport, through Leesburg, to State Highway 9, which he followed for twenty miles, passing the tiny eighteenth-century town of Hillsboro, many hilly brown fields and purple wildflowers and a few elaborate horse farms on the way to the West Virginia border. It was a magnificently rusty, golden autumn day, the kind he remembered from family car trips to see the fall wonders of Vermont.

Marty slowed his car almost to a stop at one of the huge horse farms. There was a white wooden fence around what looked like at least three acres, with stables, various houses and outbuildings, as well as an open arena dotted with several white wooden hurdles. Three people wearing fancy riding clothes and helmets were gliding horses over the hurdles. Two of the riders were obviously kids. The third was a grown woman. A mother and her two daughters . . .

Andrea and *our* two daughters? thought Marty. Maybe, someday. First I have to get her to stop hating me.

He could see them out here in the Blue Ridge, over there on those horses. They would come here on weekends and holidays, escaping from their intense public life in Washington and from their intensely active home, most probably in bipartisan Georgetown or Republican Spring Valley. Maybe Cleveland Park, with the liberal Democrats and the big-bucks pundits, if Andrea insisted. The children—maybe there should be a third, a boy—would go to St. Albans and/or NCS—National Cathedral. Here again, Andrea might insist on Sidwell Friends, and if she did, so be it. Compromise on matters such as these was crucial to their two-party marriage.

The black strip of Highway 9 curved to the left behind a row of trees and he could no longer see the horse farm, even in his rearview mirror. But he could still see his family gathered in the evening around a fireplace and a long dining-room table. There would always be good, solid talk about the issues and events that had shaped and continued to shape the nation and the world. National and international figures from the worlds of politics, philosophy, the arts, the media, religion and business would come for stimulating dinners, luncheons and on some occasions, for entire weekends.

They would all come to be part of something very special with one of America's most special couples—Senator Andrea Bartlett, Democrat, of Alaska, and Senator Martin Madigan, Republican, of Connecticut, the first husband-and-wife team ever to serve together in the United States Senate. She, a knee-jerk liberal Democrat. He, a responsible conservative Republican. Together, America at its political and personal finest.

Then, on his left, he passed a picture-book general store and service station with a large, crudely painted sign in the parking lot that warned against speeding, loitering, drinking, gambling and peeing.

And a moment later a small white-and-yellow sign on the right welcomed him to "Wild and Wonderful" West Virginia.

The highway got more hilly and curvy, the terrain became mountainous forest on both sides and the houses were fewer and much smaller and cheaper. He thought of the song John Denver or somebody sang about West Virginia but he could not remember either the tune or any of the words, except "West Virginia, take me home, take me home."

Hillmont appeared at the end of a mile-long gravel road, like a photograph in a slick country-home magazine. There on a hillside surrounded by tall, gracious trees was an absolutely magnificent three-story red-brick Georgian home. Those words from that *Baltimore Sun* story suddenly meant something to Marty. The Bennett nomination and spies and all of that aside, maybe he was going to have "a magical experience of superb elegance and time-machine history."

"Oh, Mr. Madigan, welcome to Hillmont," said a woman who met him at the door, which was dark green and appeared to have been there since the eighteenth century. "I am Mary Jane Henderson." She was in her late sixties, he guessed, and was wearing a flowing Colonial dress. From the sound of her voice she was clearly the person he had talked to on the phone. She was also clearly Mrs. Charles Avenue Henderson, wife of the warrior.

What's it like being married to a CIA warrior, Mrs. Henderson? Did he talk to you about his exploits, his hopes and fears? His glories and triumphs?

She also made Marty wonder what Andrea would look and act like when she was as old as Mrs. Henderson, an attractive, spritely woman whose age seemed strangely irrelevant to his thirty-two-year-old eyes and sensibilities.

Mrs. Henderson took him into a wide central hallway, lit by candles in brass sconces. There was the sound of recorded violin music coming from somewhere and the smell of burning wood and cooking meat and baking bread from somewhere else. It was truly like stepping through a dark green wooden door into another world, another time.

"Follow me, Mr. Madigan," Mrs. Henderson said. "I'll show you your room."

With a small suitcase in one hand, a hanging bag in the other, he walked behind her up two flights of steep stairs to a room on the third floor. It had a canopied double bed in the center and a scattering of old chairs and small tables. There was a tall armoire for his clothes and an adjoining bathroom. There were books and other reading materials on the tables but no television set or radio anywhere to be seen. Everything was clean, spare and simple.

She handed him an elegantly printed pamphlet. "Read this, Mr. Madigan, if you want to know where you are and why it matters." And she left, after inviting him to join the other guests in the front room down on the first floor for cocktails whenever he was ready. She made "cocktails" sound like the treat of a lifetime.

But there would be no cocktails for him tonight. Marty had decided on a strategy that would require his mind to be at its normal best—quick and sharp. No drinking until later in the evening, if then. Bushong's description of Henderson was responsible. Don't take on a warrior in his own lair at anything short of your best form.

He glanced at the pamphlet. It was the reprint of a *New York Times* op-ed piece about the history and beauty of this particular part of West Virginia by somebody named William Howard Adams. Marty's eye went to a quote from Thomas Jefferson about that particular place at Harpers Ferry where the Potomac and the Shenandoah Rivers come together.

Said Jefferson: "The passage of the Potowmac through the Blue Ridge is perhaps one of the most stupendous scenes in nature. You stand on a very high point of land. . . . On your right comes up the Shenandoah, having ranged along the foot of the mount an hundred miles to seek a vent. On your left approaches the Potowmac in quest of a passage also. In the moment of their junction they rush together against the mountains, rend it asunder and pass off to the sea. . . . This scene is worth a voyage across the Atlantic."

It made Marty very much want to go to Harpers Ferry and see what Jefferson saw.

But first: Charles Avenue Henderson.

Marty entered the living room, his smile as well as his quick, sharp mind at the ready. He had barely glanced at the ancient wallpaper on the walls—it looked French and handmade—

when a man dressed in a frock coat and breeches, white leggings and a wig came up to him.

"I'm Charlie Henderson," said the man.

"Marty Madigan," Marty said.

Charlie Henderson? This is Charlie Henderson, the warrior? Charlie Henderson the warrior goes around dressed up like George Washington or Thomas Jefferson?

But he was as tall as Marty and surprisingly trim and solid for a man his age. The handshake was also firm. So was his face, which was weathered but still very much alive, it seemed to Marty.

A young man in a white jacket took his drink order. Marty thought he detected a look of surprise and scorn on Charlie Henderson's face when he ordered only a soda water over ice with a slice of lemon.

He probably thinks I'm a drunk in recovery. I'm just keeping myself alert for our battle of wits, Henderson.

Mrs. Henderson, with a little help from her husband, guided him around the room to meet the other guests. There were ten in all, most of them couples in their late forties or older. Marty did a standard Washington pass-through. He made the smallest of small talk, paying little or no attention to their names or anything else about them.

And soon they were all asked to go across the hall to the dining room. Dinner was served. On with the evening, on with the business at hand.

There was one large round table in the center of the dining room, which, like the hallway, was lit by candles, on the walls and on the table. His place was between two older women. Henderson, thank God, was only one woman away on his left.

The food was absolutely spectacular.

"I have never eaten anything quite so fine," Marty said to the table about the opening event, a turtle soup. Everyone seemed to agree and the conversation went one-on-one in accordance with standard dinner-party rules.

"Is the president the fool he appears to be or is it all an act?" the woman on his left said to Marty.

Marty had worked hard for a Washington reputation as a valuable dinner-party guest. He knew what this woman was up to and he knew what was expected of him. She wanted to establish immediately that she was a serious and outspoken person. He was to acknowledge that with a serious and out-spoken response. They would then bond for an evening of serious and outspoken conversation.

"I think that kind of judgment must always be left to the individual eyes of the audience," Marty replied. It was a meaningless thing to say, exactly what he intended.

But the woman loved his answer, and she smiled and went for a large spoonful of soup.

And Marty decided to make his move on Henderson. He commented about how pleased he must be about the Bennett appointment; then, after some follow-ups about the Henderson-Bennett relationship, he referred, finally, to Jesus hats.

That one really did it.

From that moment on, Henderson never took his eyes off Marty. They were giving him a message and Marty received it: Come with me, Madigan. His words, finally spoken out in the hallway, were something about getting a breath of fresh air.

By this time Marty's head was full of second thoughts—*serious* second thoughts. Maybe he should have done the whole thing covertly, talking around it. Maybe he'd tipped his hand too soon. Maybe the whole idea of coming up here was stupid. Maybe mounting a *fake* attempt to kill the nomination of the director of Central Intelligence was even more stupid!

The air really was fresh outside. It was cool. The sky was lit by a three-quarter moon.

Marty followed Henderson away from the house, toward what appeared to be a dark thicket. He thought: The man's going to take me out here and kill me. That is what is now going to happen. I am going to die and my body will never be found. I did not tell anyone, not one soul, where I was going. They won't even know where to search for the body. My poor decaying, decomposing body.

Henderson stopped about thirty yards from the house and turned back at Marty. In the dark, Henderson seemed larger and and even more powerful than George Washington. "Who are you and what are you up to?"

Marty came to his senses. There was no way this guy was going to commit murder. Not now, not in the yard of his own house. A man as with-it as Bushong had said Henderson was would not be that stupid. Marty identified himself and his job.

Henderson moved closer—so close Marty could smell the wine and oysters on his breath. It was not a pleasant combination. The retired warrior told Marty to keep talking. He said it in a threatening way, which sounded strange coming out of the mouth of a man dressed like George Washington.

Marty said he was gathering information bearing on the confirmation of Joshua Bennett. There were some tough words between them about what might have happened with Henderson and Bennett in West Berlin.

It ended with Marty threatening a subpoena.

Even in the darkness he could sense that Henderson was going through a tremendous storm. If he really was the warrior Bushong said he was, maybe the idea of a little physical violence was not out of the question, maybe not completely off the list of possibilities at this moment.

Maybe he is stupid enough to kill me. Or at least slug me. No devious spy techniques or anything. Simply out of hate and anger he hauls off and creams me. If I survive, do I hit him back? He's thirty years older than I am. But he's a pro. I can't let him get away with slugging me. I have to fight back. But what would Simmons and the other senators think of that? They'd love it. Our guy, a Republican guy, doesn't take anything from anybody—particularly a retired spook interfering with the legitimate function of the legislative branch of government. Legitimate? Is it legitimate to be part of an internal Senate blackmail game?

Henderson turned his back on Marty, took a couple of steps away and then returned to put his face once again in Marty's. "You are now going to march back into that house, go right up to your room, gather up your belongings, come right back down, tell my wife you have a bad case of the

stomach flu, climb into your Republican car and drive your
filthy young butt out of here and out of my sight before I do
something that will make both of us sorry."

Marty, in his finest stroke of bravado, said, "We will meet
again, Mr. Henderson."

"You can count on it, friend," Henderson replied.

"You make that sound like a threat," Marty said, his voice
as firm as he could make it.

"Take it any way it fits, Mr. Madigan."

It fit as a threat.

SEVEN

Richard Crystal Winslow was exactly where Bushong's piece of paper said he would be. At 526 South Ash in Westwood, Massachusetts.

Marty had left the Hendersons' house in a rage. How dare this old spook threaten me? In threatening me he is threatening the Senate of the United States.

As George Bush said to Saddam Hussein after the Iraqi invasion of Kuwait: This will not stand.

He yelled that out loud forty-five minutes later when, instead of entering the toll road back toward his Georgetown condo, he turned off the other way to Dulles Airport.

The pocket airline directory in his briefcase said a United commuter affiliate had an 11:35 P.M. flight from Dulles to Boston. It was 11:05 when he locked his car in the long-term-parking lot and ran toward the terminal. All he carried was his small suitcase. He would have no need of the tuxedo in the hanging bag.

And here he was the next morning. Bushong's piece of paper did not say it was the address of a small motel that had been converted by a local Methodist church into a hospice for the elderly terminally ill.

Marty had no trouble talking his way past a young woman at a front desk. Mr. Winslow was in Room 129, she said, and while he seldom understood what was said, he loved to have visitors. "He has days of remarkable lucidity sometimes," she said. "If this happens to be one of those days, you're in luck."

After a walk down a narrow, gray hall that smelled of cold scrambled eggs and liquid soap he almost wished she had denied him access to this place, to this man. He tried to remind himself of the do-good thinking behind putting dying people together in one place. Why not keep them among the living for as long as possible? Or why not simply help them go ahead and die? What was the point of warehousing them in old Holiday Inns?

The man, though small and shriveled and clearly very ill, was fully dressed, propped up with pillows on top of his bedcovers, drinking a cup of black coffee and reading the sports section of *The Boston Globe*.

Marty looked first for clues as to whether this was a good day for Mr. Winslow. He checked to see if the paper was upside down. Nope. He was reading it the regular way. His clothes seemed to fit reasonably well and everything matched.

Onward. "Good morning, Mr. Winslow," he said. "Do you remember Joshua Bennett?"

There was no answer, no movement. Mr. Winslow continued to read the newspaper.

"Wasn't he a student of yours at Westwood High, Mr. Winslow?"

Winslow moved his almost bald head up and down. Progress. Good day?

"So Joshua Bennett was a student of yours, is that what you're saying?"

The paper came down with a slap.

Mr. Winslow moved his head to face Marty but otherwise remained in the same position. "Who are you?"

"Was he as great then as he is now?"

"Greater, probably. He was wonderful as a young man. I asked, Who are you?"

The voice was high and frail but every word was crisply pronounced.

"In what way was he wonderful?" Marty said.

"In every way. In every way he was wonderful. What's the point of this? Who are you? People are all the time asking me about Josh."

"He's just been nominated for a big job in Washington."

"He already has one."

"This one is even bigger."

"Congratulations."

"I'll pass that on."

"Who gives a damn what happened to him in high school?"

"Everything matters," said Marty.

"No, it doesn't," said the old man.

Marty had come with very little information or ammunition to throw into the mix as a possible prod or catalyst. He had put his mind hard to the task on the plane last night and again this morning during the one-hour ride out from the airport Marriott in his rent-a-car. He figured he had only one shot—one guess.

And the time had come.

"Taking money that doesn't belong to you always matters," he said. "No matter when, no matter by whom."

Winslow's eyes began to blink at a rapid rate. And Marty, after a few seconds of silence from the old man, decided that the window of lucidity had just closed. He had closed it with his one try, his one guess . . .

"He didn't steal for himself, he stole for his family," said Winslow finally.

"But that was a lot of money." Marty was still fishing.

Winslow went for the bait. He said, "One thousand and forty-seven dollars was a lot of money then, right. Not now. Everybody has one thousand and forty-seven dollars now."

Marty cast another line. "He went right there into your office and took it out of the safe, though."

"No, he didn't! It was the student council fund at the bank. He was president of the student council, the student body."

One more time. "Why didn't you kick him out of school or have him prosecuted, Mr. Winslow?"

The eyes were blinking again. This time not at Marty but away from him, toward a window. "I thought he learned his lesson. I thought he had a great future, and I was right, wasn't I?"

Marty asked another eight or nine questions but he got no more answers. He was at Logan Airport on his way back to Washington by late afternoon.

The flight gave him time to consider what was going on here.

Marty saw himself as a moral person. He knew the difference between right and wrong and usually did what was right. He did not lie or cheat, distort or malign. He, too, had been his high school student body president and had handled money. The idea of stealing any of it never once entered his head.

Yes, but: What were the rights and wrongs of using something like this against Bennett so many years later? Particularly in a phony attack, all in the name of water for New Mexico. Maybe it wouldn't have to *really* be used, to be made public. Either way, it was Henderson's fault. He egged us into this. Talk about immorality. He and his warrior kind reek of it. Fire must be fought with fire . . .

Marty loved debating even when, as now, he had to argue both sides. One of his favorite daydreams was of being on the floor of the United States Senate, arguing eloquently and convincingly during a dramatic confrontation over a grave matter of state—the fitness of a nominee for the Supreme Court or as secretary of state, for instance, or sending U.S. troops off to war.

Here now, on this airplane, the debate over how to use

the Bennett information did indeed concern a matter of state, but was it, he wondered, possibly even more grave for himself?

He was so engrossed in these thoughts that it was only when the plane began its final approach to Washington, one hour and ten minutes after takeoff, that he even noticed the unopened snack box and small bottle of white wine on the tray table in front of him.

He awoke in his own bed in his own place in the Tannery and did what he usually did on Sunday morning. Without shaving or showering, he threw on some rough clothes, walked across the footbridge to Dean & Deluca and had a cinnamon coffee, a peach danish and both *The New York Times* and *The Washington Post*. It was the only ritual in his life.

He wondered if Andrea would understand such a thing, go along with it, join him in it. Would she want to jump out of bed and do this with him? What would he do if she didn't? Could he compromise this away in the interests of peace and love? Should these kinds of things be worked out in advance?

And on and on the questions came. The problem—and it was a major one when he came upon it—was that he had been there at that small table in the covered D&D patio for almost an hour before those questions popped into his mind. What was an even larger problem was that Andrea Bartlett, the woman with whom he had decided to live the perfect American political life, had not popped into his mind at all since shortly before he walked through that green door at Hillmont on Friday night. Now it was Sunday morning. He would call Andrea later today. Yes, of course, he would. But for now it was back to what had been in his mind since he left Mr. Winslow at that hospice.

How can I go after a guy for stealing one thousand forty-seven dollars when he was in high school? Is that fair? Is that the way the game of advise and consent should be played in the United States Senate? But, remember, this game is not the game it appears to be. I wouldn't really be going after Bennett because it would never come to that. Still, even so, just bringing up something that happened thirty-five years ago when the guy was seventeen years old doesn't seem right. I cannot let my annoyance with that old spook in the George Washington suit cloud my judgment and sense of fairness.

But. On the other hand. Wait a minute.

What about the idea that patterns in a person's life are established early and never change? What about those expense vouchers Bushong gave him? What do they really mean? Do they mean once a thief, always a thief? Has Bennett been cheating and stealing while an employee of the Central Intelligence Agency? Is he a born thief, a man who can't keep from stealing? Should such a man be the DCI? Should our opposition to Bennett be real?

He needed to get another name from Bushong.

Bushong, the Republicans' favorite CIA man, had set up a silly spy-novel way for Republicans to get in touch with him on weekends. Marty followed it because he had no choice. He assumed he lived in McLean, Falls Church or one of the other Virginia suburbs close to Langley, but that was only an assumption. He had neither an address nor a phone number.

So Marty went to a pay phone at the corner of Wisconsin and O Street in central Georgetown. Per procedure, it was a pay phone he had never used before. He called a number and got a recorded electronically distorted female voice that said: "This number is a nonworking number. Please call 202-555-8943 for further information." He called the second number. A male voice said only: "Please leave your name and number and your call will be returned." Marty said: "This is Barry. The cake is ready. My number is 202-555-7775." He then hung up, glanced at his watch and walked briskly to a phone inside the mall at Georgetown Park, six blocks away. He went to the pay phone with the number 202-555-7775, which he had copied down earlier, and picked up the receiver. He faked talking in order to keep the phone free and then, when fifteen minutes had gone by after his first calls, he hung up. And within five seconds, the phone rang.

"Did you follow the recipe?" Bushong said, meaning did he follow the telephone procedures. It was also a double-check code.

"I had trouble with the icing," Marty said.

"Everyone does."

OK, I know you, what is it? was what that meant.

"I need somebody who can make sense of those expense papers."

Bushong did not answer.

After a few beats of silence Marty said, "Did you hear me?"

"I did," Bushong said. "I know who you need. She's retired, gone, I have to find her. You want it now, today?"

"Yes."

"Why?"

"Because I work better when I'm on a roll, and I'm on a roll."

"Where will you be in one hour?"

"Wherever you want me to be."

There was another brief silence before Bushong said, "In exactly one hour go to the rear of the Washington Cathedral, walk up the left side aisle in the main sanctuary to the fifth pew. Turn right and go in to the third seat. Sit down. Feel under the seat on the right-hand side. You will find what you want."

"Come on, Russ, is playing these games really necessary? Why not just call me?"

There was a note of disgust in Bushong's voice when he said, "Necessary isn't the test anymore, Marty. It's the fun part of this kind of work that keeps us all going now that the KGB is gone and Ames ruined it all. These 'games,' as you call them, are all we have left. Play them, Marty. Play them, love them, enjoy them."

Marty wasn't sure he was really loving and enjoying the games he was playing at this moment with Bushong, a self-promoting jerk who probably had no business working in the intelligence service of the United States of America. But Marty kept quiet.

And exactly an hour later he was at the corner of Wisconsin and Massachusetts Avenues moving down the left aisle of the Washington Cathedral, the place past and present D.C. dignitaries went for funerals and similar events that required a stately and religious setting. Somebody up front was playing "A Mighty Fortress Is Our God" on the organ—practicing, apparently, for a future service. Marty paid little attention. He also barely looked at the statue of Abraham Lincoln or the spectacular stained-glass windows or any of the cathedral's other attractions. He was not there as a tourist.

But as he left the cathedral a few minutes later with a piece of paper in his pocket it occurred to him that this would be the perfect place for his and Andrea's wedding. Absolutely the perfect place.

It was an Episcopal church, though. That would be fine with him, but what about Andrea? She couldn't be Catholic, could she? Or Jewish? Not that it would matter to him. His mother, head of the vestry at St. James Episcopal Church back home, wouldn't even care. Thank God your religion didn't matter that much anymore. Except in Northern Ireland, of course. And Bosnia and Iran and places like that, where it can get you killed.

His attention went now to what was in the envelope.

"Careful. She hates people like us."

That was what somebody—presumably Bushong—had typed underneath the name, address and phone number on the piece of paper he had retrieved from under the pew.

Us? Why does she hate people like us?

The name was Carla L. Avery. Her address was a place

called White Rapids, West Virginia. He recognized 304, her area code, as the same as the one he called to make his Hillmont reservation.

What is this about West Virginia? Is that where all old spooks go to die?

He found White Rapids on the map he pulled from the glove compartment of his car. Damned if it wasn't also in the Panhandle. Damned if it wasn't only ten miles or so from Charles Town.

Suddenly, the idea of driving back up there right now—it was after three o'clock—made him tired. And he felt the rhythm and energy go out of that roll he was on.

But back at his place at the Tannery a short while later he had second thoughts. Move while it's hot. Get on with it. But he would call first. He would tell Carla L. Avery something and make an appointment. If not for tonight, then for some day next week. He wouldn't tell her what he was up to, but would say it involved a matter of government importance. Should he give his name? Those former spooks probably stick together up there. She might immediately call Henderson. No, no names. He would think of some cover story . . .

But he didn't have to. He called that 304 number five times at roughly thirty-minute intervals over the course of the evening and all he got was an unanswered ring.

That is also what he got when he remembered to call Andrea Bartlett, his future wife and the future senator from Alaska. It was almost ten o'clock. He wondered where in the world she was this late on a Sunday night. Didn't she watch *Masterpiece Theatre*?

The thought of *Masterpiece Theatre* made him laugh. He couldn't remember the last time *he* had had the time—had taken the time, at least—to sit down in front of a television set to watch any non-news program as long as an hour. Except for movies. Sometimes late at night when he couldn't sleep he would watch a movie—most of them, it seemed, starring Bruce Willis performing various acts of violence.

What does Andrea do when she can't sleep?

Marty left a telephone message with Andrea Bartlett's secretary at eleven-thirty the next morning. He had meant to call earlier but he got distracted by other things, such as getting multiple copies made of various documents and statements that would be used in the hearing and meeting with members of the majority staff. He avoided talking to Senator Simmons because it was too early to lay out anything. He also did not talk to Carla Avery because there was still no answer at that 304 number. He decided to give it a while longer before going back to Bushong.

It was just after four o'clock that afternoon when a call from Henderson put him back on a roll.

"I'm ready to tell you about Berlin," Henderson said. "I'm a good citizen, I believe in acting like one."

Marty said he was delighted to hear that.

Henderson said, "Sorry about throwing you out the other night, too. Josh Bennett and I go back a long way. I let my personal feelings get in the way of my duty. I'm sorry."

"Your apologies are accepted. Friendship is important."

It was Henderson's suggestion that Marty come up to West Virginia for their meeting late the next morning. He suggested a room over a restaurant called the Yellow Brick Bank in a place called Shepherdstown and gave Marty the directions.

"It'll be quiet and private so we can really talk," Henderson said.

Marty was sure much of what the man had said was pure lie. But he was not sure how much, and the only way to find out was to go in the morning to a yellow brick bank in West Virginia.

He might also use the opportunity to swing by White Rapids afterward and see what signs he could turn up of the woman who hated people like him.

Then Andrea returned his call.

"How was your weekend in West Virginia?" she asked.

"Mixed. And yours?"

"I just worked."

"I thought you had a date."

"That was Saturday night."

"How was it?"

"Fine. We went to a black-tie dinner, like I said."

"Do you like black-tie dinners?"

"They're all the same. Old men talking too long about themselves and each other."

"Do you ride horses?"

"Never."

"What did you do last night?"

"I went out with a friend from the office. A woman friend. We went to a movie. I like movies."

"Have you ever watched *Masterpiece Theatre?*"

"Sometimes. But mostly it's too British for me."

They agreed to try to have lunch on Wednesday or Thursday.

And they hung up. Then Marty remembered something else. He called her right back, she came on the line and he said, "What did you do yesterday morning?"

"It was Sunday. I don't do anything on Sunday mornings but read the papers, drink coffee, lie around. I don't even comb my hair until after noon."

"You don't go to church?"

"No."

"Which one would you go to if you did?"

"Marty, what in the hell are you doing? You want to know what my religion is?"

"Well, not really . . ."

"This sounds like some kind of matchmaking interview. Forget it, OK?"

"I'm sorry, I really am. I couldn't care less what you are. I just want to know how do you feel about the Washington Cathedral?"

"Good-bye, Marty."

Marty hung up the phone after first considering banging it against his head a few times. I really must do better than this or there will never be a wedding at the Washington Cathedral or anywhere else.

He concluded that it was the Bennett/Faucet/Henderson business. It was distracting him, rattling him, obsessing him. When it was over, he would do better.

. . .

Marty made an opening crack about how different Henderson looked in a brown tweed jacket than in a George Washington suit. Henderson did not bother to fake even a small grin.

The place really was yellow. And it had obviously been a bank in an earlier life. Downstairs it was now a restaurant; upstairs there were three hotel-like rooms, in one of which he was now sitting with Charles Avenue Henderson. And with who knows what kind of sophisticated electronic recording devices.

Marty decided to get on with it. He asked Henderson to tell him the whole story of West Berlin, as he'd said he would.

Henderson began: "Certainly. I'll be glad to. But I would like to know first exactly what it is you and your colleagues are up to. How would my information be used and by whom?" So, Marty realized, it's a setup. He played along.

"The Constitution calls for the Senate of the United States to advise and consent on presidential appointees. That's what this is all about. The president has nominated your friend Bennett to be director of Central Intelligence and we are—"

Henderson, speaking obviously for the hidden recording device as well as to him, interrupted and got nasty. He told Marty to cut the shit because he didn't have time to waste.

"Yes, Mr. Henderson, I guess it must be pretty taxing dressing up like George Washington every weekend."

Dramatically, like a bad actor in a bad forties movie, Henderson leaped up. "End of clandestine meeting, end of your games, Mr. Madigan," he declared.

Clandestine meeting? This is about as clandestine as an Oprah Winfrey show.

Marty, enjoying himself more than he would have imagined possible in such a situation, remained seated. He dropped his voice to a near whisper and suggested to Henderson that what lay before them with the Bennett nomination had the potential of becoming a national security catastrophe.

Henderson sat back down. Marty raised the volume for what he said next.

"What if I told you we have information that shows Joshua Eugene Bennett to be a thief. An old-fashioned kind of thief. The kind who steals money that belongs to others and who has been doing it for years."

"I do not believe that!"

Marty could not tell about Henderson. Was he really upset? Was it all a show? Was he just a simpleminded old spy standing with an old friend for old times' sake? Or was he an evil bastard playing evil games with the Senate of the United States and thus with the security of the United States?

Who is the coolest one of all in this room above a yellow brick bank?

They exchanged some posturing words, ending with Marty accusing Henderson of having the room bugged under the direction of, and for the benefit of, Joshua Bennett himself.

Marty was hungry. It was almost noon.

"What's the food like downstairs?" he said to Henderson as he headed for the door.

"Try the bean soup and the Caesar salad." Henderson said it without a second of hesitation. Life goes on even when the country is faced with a potential national security disaster.

Marty Madigan felt good about himself as he ate his lunch. Henderson had been right about the Cuban black bean soup and the Caesar salad. Both were terrific.

He had been pretty terrific, too, as a player of Henderson's game. The thought gave him an unexpected sense of well-being, much like the one he got when he jogged or saw a terrific piece of sculpture.

White Rapids was a town of maybe ten short streets and about thirty dwellings, mostly frame houses, that looked to be at least fifty years old. On the main road through town, there were also a Mobil station, a furniture-refinishing place, an antique store, a small grocery that also rented videos and an income tax service.

The house at the address on Bushong's piece of paper was a two-story white frame that was clean, freshly painted and quite large. A graceful full porch came around the front from halfway back on both sides. The house had a look of peace and friendliness and comfort to it.

There was no answer at the door. Marty knocked several times, waiting at least a minute before knocking again. He listened carefully for some noise inside. He heard none.

Nobody was home. Carla L. Avery did not answer her phone because she wasn't there. But there were no newspapers on the porch and the mailbox on the right side of the door was empty. And generally he got the feeling that people had been there recently and regularly.

"You looking for Carla?"

It was a woman's voice. Marty turned with a start. As satisfied as he was with how he'd dealt with Henderson, he was still a bit jumpy about all of this.

Off the porch on the left side stood a gray-haired woman in blue jeans and a red-and-yellow plaid shirt. She looked as if she had been interrupted while doing something even she thought was not terribly important.

"Yes, ma'am, I am," Marty said. "Hello there. Yes, I am looking for Carla."

"She's down at her office. It's tax time for some people, you know. End of the fiscal year or some nonsense like that. I used to think it was only April fifteenth we had to worry about. She's there at her office night and day right now."

"Oh, yes. Certainly. I should have known."

The woman disappeared and so did Marty.

"All-American Tax Service" said the small red-white-and-blue sign on a kind of marquee above the door. Below it, in smaller black print, was the declaration "Dedicated to Helping You Keep As Much As You Can."

There was a jingle of a bell when he opened the door. The Yellow Brick Bank Restaurant had been a bank. This place looked as if it might have been a movie theater or an opera house in its earlier life. Inside, the floor began a slant downward. At the windowless end of the slant sat a woman behind a long table bearing stacks of paper and twin green-shaded table lamps.

"If you want your return done, I can only do it with an extension. No way I can get it done by the deadline. Just look around."

She said all of this without really looking at him. He walked closer to her and the table.

"I was here to talk about something else," he said.

"Too busy to talk about anything else," she said.

"I apologize for the timing but it's about a matter of national security."

He saw her face now for the first time. It was round and pockmarked. She was wearing large black-rimmed glasses over very green eyes. He didn't know what color her hair had been earlier in life, but now it was almost white and was pinned back and up in a large bun.

"I haven't heard talk like that in a long time," she said. "Who in the hell are you?"

"My name is Martin Madigan. I work on the staff of the Senate Select Committee on Intelligence."

"What are you doing here?"

"I came to see you."

"I hate people like you."

"That's what I was told."

"By whom?"

Marty had to make a decision. To name or not name? He had an immediate and certain feeling that a refusal to name his source would end this meeting. Just like that.

"Russ Bushong."

"I hate that sunavabitch."

She motioned toward a wooden folding chair off to his right. He grabbed it quickly and moved it up to the table, directly across from her.

"As you may have read, Joshua Bennett has been nominated by the president to be DCI."

"He's a sunavabitch, too. They all are."

"Didn't you work closely with Bennett at one time?"

"You know that already or you wouldn't be here."

"True."

"You must be a Republican."

"I am."

"You want dirt."

"Not dirt necessarily. Just the truth."

She let out an exasperated sigh. And for a moment he thought he had blown it. She gestured with both hands at the stacks of papers on both sides of her and behind her and just about everywhere else in that large room.

"Spit it out, young man. My time is money."

"Money is what I want to talk about. Money that Josh Bennett got for travel and other work expenses. I have information which says he cheated and he cheated badly and often. I understand he faked vouchers and other things—"

The phone rang. She let it ring twice before answering with a terse "Taxes."

Marty watched her listen. She grunted and frowned.

"I hear you," she said after a couple of minutes and hung up.

Marty decided to remain silent. She clearly knew what he wanted. It was up to her now to decide whether or not he got it.

"You know why I know what you want to know about Bennett?" she said finally.

"Not really, no, ma'am."

"It's because that is all those bastards would let me do. I was screened and hired and trained to be a covert operator just like they were. I had all of the language skills they had, I could shoot a .45 and handle myself physically as well as they could. But they made me take care of their goddamn travel arrangements and expense forms on the grounds that I needed to learn it all from the ground up. They treated me like I was their goddamn secretary at first. And then they graduated me into reading intercepted mail from students studying Russian at places like Southeast Kansas State Teachers College, and then to keeping fourth assistant military attachés at Russian embassies under surveillance. I never ever got to do anything that mattered. I hated those bastards then, every goddamn one of them, I hate them now and I will go to my grave hating them."

She stopped talking and angrily ripped the top sheet off a small memo pad. Then, with her right hand, she slowly crumpled up the piece of paper as if it were a piece of a one of those bastards she hated so much.

Now what? thought Marty. Should I repeat my question about Bennett and the expenses? Should I just grunt? Should I express outrage over the way she was treated, express support and appreciation for her plight? Yes, that is what I will do.

"That is outrageous!" he said angrily and much too loudly. "They should have been dismissed from the Agency. The same thing happened to Sandra Day O'Connor when she got out of law school. No law firm would hire her except as a secretary—"

"Oh, shut up," she said. "If you had been there you would have done the same thing. All men in the Agency treated all women that way. Except foreign women. The warrior boys loved to work with Turkish women and French women and German women and Pakistani women, even Russian women. It was only American women who were not good enough for these smug, arrogant cowboys who thought they ruled the universe. So shut up."

He shut up.

She stood and walked back and forth behind her huge table a few times. She was about five six by Marty's estimate, a woman who moved well and, like Charlie Henderson's wife, was splendidly maintained for somebody in her late sixties. Was she a runner? And what was she doing here in West Virginia? If she hated the old boys so much, why did she live right in the middle of them?

Marty decided to try talking again. "Was Charles Henderson one of them?"

Still standing, she stopped and looked right at him. "You bet he was."

"I guess . . . well, you must know he lives not fifteen minutes from here."

"Yes, I must know that. That was him on the phone just now."

Oh, my God. "Well, well, now. I don't know what to say. I just came from meeting with him up over a restaurant . . ."

"He told me. He told me what you are up to. He told me Josh Bennett would be a great DCI. He suggested I might want to put any old hates behind me."

She started her pacing again.

Marty waited a few minutes before saying something that might again stop her in her tracks. He tried, "If you detest these guys so much, what are you doing living up here? Bushong said there were several—"

"Good question, Mr. Republican. I am not a Republican, by the way. In fact, I'm about as far from being a Republican as it is possible to be and still be on the charts. You're like the warriors. You are smug and arrogant. You think you have all the answers. You have none of the answers because you have none of the questions."

She took a breath and said, "The answer is in this building and that house where I live. I came here to live with my husband after he retired. He was a warrior, a China-hand warrior. He got shot in the back in Shanghai and became a Blue Heart and a half invalid. He couldn't go back out into the field so he switched to intelligence assessment—a Langley desk job—and I quit the Agency, took some courses and became an accountant of sorts. My husband died two years ago. We had a wonderful life here in the Panhandle. It is the single most wonderful place in the world to live. Go over to Harpers Ferry and stand on Jefferson's Rock if you want to see for yourself. I mostly ignored Henderson and the others while Roy was alive—Roy was my husband. Ex-spies are the best people to live among because they understand privacy. Roy enjoyed being around them because he never had to explain anything, including how he got hurt. Specifically, what do you want to know about Bennett?"

"How he stole and how much."

Carla Avery crossed her arms. Her eyes took on a new glistening. This was her story to tell and, finally, she was telling it. "He had a desk drawer full of blank receipts, hotel, restaurant, rental-car and other kinds. Every time he made a legitimate trip he would come back with pads of receipts with the real names of real places printed on them. Then every so often he would get me or somebody else to fill them out and he'd turn them in. It was easy. The Agency then was completely dependent on its people being honest. The ethic was that it was not right to question people who were risking their lives for their country. If an agent said he rented five cars in three days and took seven people to seven different dinners on the same night, so be it."

"How much money was involved?" Marty asked again.

"I didn't run a total on an adding machine," she said. "But if I had to guess I'd say it was a couple of thousand a year."

"How many years?"

"Seven that I was involved in."

"So about fifteen thousand in all—that you know about?"

"At least."

"Did Henderson do it, too?"

"No, no. I think Bennett did it because he had some personal family problems. He didn't use the money to buy fancy cars and things the way Ames did. That was one of the reasons Bennett never got caught. He never bought anything. I hated myself for loving it that Ames got away with it for so long the way he did."

Ames was a Soviet spy! Marty wanted to shout. He sold out his country—not just a few fellow warriors at the CIA. People *died* because of what he did, for God's sake.

Marty said none of this. All he cared about right now was Joshua Bennett.

"What caused Bennett to stop stealing?"

"Charlie Henderson stopped him."

"How?"

"He told Bennett to stop it or he would turn him in."

EIGHT

Marty believed some of his success in life thus far could be attributed to the coherence and logic of what emerged from his various word processors through various laser-jet printers onto the printed page. He knew, for instance, that he could take what he had learned from the files Bushong had slipped him and from Carla Avery and from Richard Adams Winslow, toss it all around and emerge with a dramatic and persuasive case for not confirming Joshua Eugene Bennett as director of Central Intelligence. He worked most of Tuesday night at his apartment and much of Wednesday behind his closed office door doing that very thing.

"You really are the best," said Senator Simmons after glancing through a one-page synopsis of Marty's forty-one-page single-spaced confidential, Eyes-Senator-Only memo.

"Thank you, sir," Marty replied.

"Nothing in the clips yet about this, I see."

"Everybody is still expecting smooth sailing for the nomination," Marty said. "What about the subpoena of Henderson, Senator?"

"What about it?"

It was mid-morning on Thursday and they were in one of the Senators-Only elevators in the Capitol. A water aide and a press aide with the clips had left them on the first floor, a grazing aide would meet them on the third. They had a two-floor trip to have their private conference about what most people in the office now referred to as the Bennett matter.

Marty quickly recited the facts and the need for subpoenaing Henderson. "The papers requesting the subpoena are here," said Marty. "You sign them and I will take them to majority staff and get the rest of it processed. With a little luck it could be served on Henderson by tonight."

Simmons signed just as the elevator arrived at the third floor. "I told Grover we were on track," Simmons said. "Should I give him your memo?"

"No, sir," Marty said. "That should remain my eyes only for now. There may come a time to use it but not now. We don't want to signal too much, too soon."

"Right, right. We need to talk through my statements and strategy for the hearing itself. There's never time to do everything, Marty, but we'll find it. You're doing a good job on this Bennett matter. You really are. I hope it works. For the sake of water in my state, I hope it works. We're having dinner with the Bushongs tonight. Anything you need me to get from him? He loves to tell me secrets. Any we need?"

"Can't think of a one, Senator," Marty said, giving him a half wave as Simmons stepped off quickly down the hall with the grazing aide.

Marty spent the rest of the day thinking mostly of the possibility of seeing Andrea Bartlett that night. She had agreed to at least consider meeting him at nine o'clock for a drink. She had much work to do on a Mississippi River barges appropriations bill, and it was unlikely she could meet him, but at his insistence she said she would hold open the possibility. They agreed on the bar at another chic Italian restaurant, Madeo on Northwest Twenty-second Street, a few blocks east of Georgetown.

Marty did not really expect her to show up, but he was there at eight fifty-five. He ordered a Perrier with lime and continued to think about her.

Nine o'clock came and went without a sign of her and so did nine-fifteen.

At nine twenty-five he got a telephone call at the bar from Senator Simmons. Intimidated by Jane Culver, Marty had told the office where he was going to be this evening.

The senator was speaking in a voice as close to a screech as Marty had ever heard from a grown man. "There's been an emergency! Something terrible has happened! Come to my house—right now!"

Five minutes later Marty was at the senator's house on N Street. It was a three-story red brick Georgian that, like so many Georgetown houses, had a history of past owners from the Washington world of politics and government. Every time he was there, Marty was impressed with the fact that, going back to the mid-1880s, a secretary of state, a *Washington Post* executive editor, one of the columnist Alsop brothers and four U.S. senators had lived here.

Now, the fifth senator stood before him, looking shaken and upset. Simmons's face was flushed, his tie was away from his collar, his hair was messed up.

And his words came tumbling out in a semibabble Marty had never before heard from him.

"We were there in one of the back tables. Sally and me, Russ and Eloise. We love Nora's. Liberals own it, I think, but the food is healthy and tasty. They do a lot of that free-range-chicken and fruit-sorbet sort of thing. We came in Russ's car, that brown Jaguar of his. He calls it mahogany rather than brown. Nice, very nice. He parked it within a few feet of the front door at a fire hydrant. Even I don't do that with my New Mexico senator's plates. But Russ said there would be no problem, he could park anywhere he wanted, any time he wanted. CIA people still amaze me sometimes, Marty, they really do. How in the world would a D.C. cop know that Jag belonged to a CIA man who was inside Nora's eating free-range chicken?"

It's because of purple dots, Marty could have said, almost said. Later. He would explain that to the senator later. Right now all he wanted to know was what in the hell had happened.

"We were only halfway through the main course—I had the grilled Chilean sea bass on a lentil ragout, not the chicken, as a matter of fact—when there was one hell of an explosion. I mean really loud and jarring. It rocked me back from the table and our wineglasses almost tipped over and I thought the roof might fall in on us. It was scary, Marty. As scary as it gets. A lot of people screamed. I heard windows rattling and the sound of glass and other things breaking. In a few seconds we realized it was outside, which was a relief but not much. Russ was cool. Without really looking up from his dinner—I don't remember now what he was eating, but I think it was the Maine lobster bruschetta with some kind of caviar sauce—he said something about it being an explosive, probably plastique. I suggested that maybe one of us—meaning him because he was the professional, after all— might want to go see what happened. He said, forget it, it wasn't his jurisdiction."

Simmons's face was flushed, even more so than after a good run around the Georgetown track.

"So we kept on eating. We just kept on eating. Sally, bless her heart, hadn't screamed. She had barely blanched, in fact. Same with Eloise. All part of going out to eat at night in Washington, D.C., our nation's capital. The National Guard will be patroling the streets of this place before long. I'm serious. It could come to that. It would probably be illegal and set precedents none of us want, but I smell it coming. I really do."

Marty noticed Simmons's right hand was shaking. Another first.

"I was sitting facing the front of the place, toward the entrance. We went on talking about the explosion. Russ said it might even have been a water main. He said he might have been wrong about the plastique. After the Czechs got out of the explosives-manufacturing business when Havel came in, there wasn't as much of that stuff around as there used to be. Did you know, Marty, that most of the plastique used in bombs was made in Czechoslovakia? Make a note for us to look into where it's coming from now. Libya, I bet. Or Syria or North Korea. Might make for an interesting hearing, although, God knows, the one thing I do not need right now is another hearing to go to. I went to twelve different ones today, Marty. Twelve. Some of them I was just there to introduce somebody from New Mexico. But some of them I actually had to stay and ask questions. Forget about the plastique explosives things. The people of New Mexico could not care less where some Muslim crazy gets his goddamn bomb parts."

The senator went suddenly silent. He stood up and walked over to the bar in a corner of the room, which was a study lined with political books and dozens of framed photographs of Simmons accepting or presenting everything from trophies to handshakes in the company of prominent public people.

He poured three inches of scotch into a glass and added nothing to it. Not even ice. He drank it all in two large swallows, without offering anything to Marty, an act of bad manners that Marty had never before seen the senator commit.

"I heard the sound of sirens outside and in a minute or

two after that I saw the manager of the place making the rounds. He was asking questions at each table and then moving on. Finally he got to us. 'Excuse me,' he said. 'We're looking for someone who might have been driving a Jaguar XJ6 parked just outside. On the R Street side. I think it's a dark brown, but it's hard to tell. It has just blown itself apart.' It has just blown itself apart. That is what he said. A brown Jaguar XJ6 had just blown itself apart."

Marty had to fight off a growing desire to shake along with Simmons. And wanting three inches of scotch or something similar.

"Marty, I looked right at Russ Bushong. He was directly across from me at the table, which was square. I thought his face was going to blow apart. He screamed something about Bennett and Henderson. I thought—seriously, Marty—that he was going to have a heart attack right there at the table. Or a stroke at least. It was a terrible thing to see. I wondered if I could remember exactly how to do CPR. I learned how to do it a few years ago. So did Sally. The Red Cross or somebody launched a big campaign to teach it to everyone in New Mexico. We came in as the first students to bring attention to it. There were stories in the papers and on television. It is amazing the number of things like that I am asked to do. I wish I could spend more time on the issues and on subjects like intelligence and foreign policy and defense. But that is not what the people of New Mexico sent me here to do. Ask Fulbright. Ask Percy. Ask Foley. Ask a lot of guys who came here to save the world and discovered it was only the states of Arkansas or Illinois that their voters had in mind for saving. That's why I'm still here and they're not."

Speaking those words of triumph and survival seemed to abruptly change things. Marty watched the red leave the senator's face and a steadiness return to his right hand and the empty glass grasped in it.

Marty said, "Bennett and Henderson? Are you sure Bushong said those two names?"

In a firm, senatorial voice, Simmons said, "Yes. Isn't Henderson the one I signed the subpoena on this afternoon? Isn't it about the Bennett matter? Didn't you say they would probably have it served by tonight?"

Marty confirmed all points.

"What's going on, Marty? Are there people aligned with Bennett and the CIA seeking to influence a decision of the Senate of the United States through acts of terrorism? And if so, are we—Sally and me . . . and you, even—in any kind of danger?"

The shaking was gone from Simmons but not the fear. "I doubt it," Marty said. "There is no telling how many problems—and enemies—Bushong has created in the course of his life."

"But he yelled out the names of those two—Bennett and Henderson. The clips will probably be full of this in the morning."

Marty, for some reason, doubted that. But he said, "Yes, sir."

"Who exactly *is* Henderson?" Simmons asked.

"I don't know, sir." It was a reflexively protective answer. Marty didn't want to talk to Simmons about Henderson. Not now, not tonight.

It was only afterward, out on N Street walking away from

that famous Georgetown house, that Marty realized—and rationalized—that his answer was probably not even a lie.

Marty looked up from unlocking his car in the Tannery parking garage the next morning. Russell Bushong was standing next to him. It was only seven-thirty.

"Those sunsabitches blew up my XJ6, Madigan," Bushong said.

Marty probably imagined it, but he swore he saw tears in the man's eyes. Plus a lot of hate and loathing.

"I know, the senator told me," Marty said. "But it wasn't in the paper this morning."

"It'll never be in the paper."

Were there purple dots for *Washington Post* stories, too?

"I want Bennett destroyed," Bushong said, as if he were Patton addressing the Third Army. "I want him crushed into little pieces of dead meat. I want him not only not to get the big job, I want him out on his ass from the job he has now. I want him ruined and humiliated, shamed and profaned. Nobody blows up an XJ6 of mine and survives."

Marty resisted snapping a Yes, sir! salute. "We're working on it," he said as calmly as he could.

"Bullshit." Marty felt a slight sprinkle of spittle. Bushong was right up in his face.

Marty said, "Hey, come on. We have a deal. I give you Bennett, you give me a purple dot."

"Bullshit."

"I saw Winslow and Avery. It's coming together. He told me the story about high school. She told me about the phony receipts. We've subpoenaed Henderson about the Blue Heart story in Berlin. We'll put him under oath, he'll talk."

"What dreamworld did you wake up in this morning?"

"It'll be all right," Marty said, his voice so low he wasn't sure Bushong even heard him.

The fact was: No, no. It, of course, would not be all right. Not to this man Bushong, the man you are now telling lies to. And you *are* lying to him. Bennett is not going to be destroyed. Everything that has been turned up on him will be used to get a Texas senator's friend a judgeship and the people of New Mexico some water. None of the bad stuff will see the light of day, Bennett will be confirmed as DCI and everyone, including him, will live happily ever after. Sorry about your XJ6, Bushong. You are absolutely right about it being bullshit but you don't know how right. Or do you?

Whatever, at this particular moment Marty had to keep the lies alive. "Is there anything else you can tell us about Bennett?" he asked Bushong, who had, at least, moved back a step.

"I don't think Simmons really cares about getting Bennett," Bushong said, ignoring the question. "At dinner last night, before Bennett's sunsabitches blew up my car, I got the impression Lank Simmons is up to something. What is it, Madigan? All he talked about was water and trees, shit like that."

"Do you have anything else you can give us on Josh Bennett?"

"Yes. I'll give it to you later if you promise to use it. Something about this smells, Madigan."

Everything about this smells, thought Marty. As of now,

the only person or thing to get hurt has been a mahogany-brown XJ6 Jaguar with a purple dot on its license plate. He had the shivering thought that this could change.

He asked Bushong why Bennett and Henderson would do something as stupid and risky as blowing up his car.

"They know me and my feelings about my car. They wanted to send a message about helping you against Bennett. It's that simple."

Simple? Marty made a minispeech about how outrageous, illegal and intolerable it was, and he urged Bushong to go to the press and get the D.C. police or whoever to vigorously investigate and prosecute these guys who thought they were above the law.

Bushong, now leaning against a fender of Marty's car, gave no sign that he heard a word of it. He changed the subject. "Henderson told me you fingered me. He said you gave him the whole story about how I was giving you everything I could find on Bennett."

"That's not true! I hope to hell you don't for one minute believe I would tell Henderson or anyone else anything like that . . ."

Marty wasn't sure how much of any of that last part Bushong heard. By the time he had finished, Bushong was ten feet away, walking off with his back to him.

And it wasn't until he had driven his car to another underground parking lot—the one under the Senate side of the U.S. Capitol—that Marty noticed the thick white envelope on the right front seat. He opened it as he walked out of the garage. There was an audiocassette inside. Obviously Bushong had been in the Tannery garage for a while. But how did he get into the locked car and out again without leaving a trace?

It was a recording of a telephone conversation between two men. Marty listened to the tape on a small cassette player in his office behind a closed and locked door. He easily recognized one of the voices as that of Charles Avenue Henderson. He had no idea about the other except that Henderson called him Scotty.

HENDERSON: The bastards served a subpoena on me tonight.

SCOTTY: Do you know what time it is, for Christ's sake? I am an old and tired man, Henderson. I need my sleep before I sleep.

HENDERSON: I'm an old man, too, Scotty.

SCOTTY: Nobody is as old a man as I am. What does the subpoena demand of you?

HENDERSON: Appear in two days in Room 215 of the Hart Senate Office Building at the Capitol in Washington prepared to answer questions.

SCOTTY: We discussed this possibility. Why are you calling at such a desperate hour in such a desperate manner?

HENDERSON: Mr. Mix also shredded the Ralston tonight.

SCOTTY: So a busy night all around in the conspiracy business, I see.

HENDERSON: Exactly.

SCOTTY: But again, the shredding came as no surprise to anyone, except, of course, the nincompoop who owned same. What, pray tell, is your goddamn problem?

HENDERSON: Will you go with me to Washington?

SCOTTY: For companionship, old man, or what?

HENDERSON: As my lawyer.

SCOTTY: Oh, Brother Henderson, you are indeed a man of bravery and risk. I am no longer in a position to do anyone any good. I am a man and mind of the past. Please, please. Do not ask, so that I will not have to even think about it.

HENDERSON: I'm asking.

SCOTTY: The answer is yes.

HENDERSON: Thank you.

SCOTTY: No, it is I who thanks you.

HENDERSON: For what?

SCOTTY: For asking. Never call me again on the phone about this.

HENDERSON: I don't care if they hear this.

SCOTTY: It's not this that I am concerned about. It's what we may say or plan for the future. Our next target may be a facility much larger and more important than some mahogany-brown Ralston of show and pretension. We would not want the little people who listen to other people's telephone conversations to know our plans in advance.

HENDERSON: Good point, Scotty.

SCOTTY: Your praise truly matters to me on matters of this kind.

They said good-bye and there was the sound of two phones hanging up.

Marty immediately picked up the one on his desk and got Bushong on the phone at the CIA. There was no spy funny business, just a straight phone call on an open line.

"Who is the other guy?" Marty asked.

"Scotty Hartman is his name. He was general counsel here for a long time. He did other things before that. He's mean and smart and he's very fat and very old."

"We've got 'em dead on the bombing. Did you hear that stuff about mahogany brown and other targets?"

"That was for our benefit, Madigan. They know nobody could prove a thing."

"Why not?"

"Because it was done by people who do not leave proof."

"What about the D.C. police? Aren't they working on it?"

"They couldn't find a bear in a zoo."

Marty was confused. "Why was what was said on that tape for us? I don't get it."

"Just in case we were listening, they wanted us to know they knew we were listening. It's pure Hartman and Henderson. They're tough stuff, Madigan. Remember what I said to you the other day about fun? These guys helped invent the fun parts."

"They're goddamn terrorists!"

"Yes, indeed. And aren't you, in fact, feeling a little terrorized?"

Marty, in fact, did not answer.

The man introduced himself and handed Marty a small white calling card. A name was printed in bold black type in the center. JONATHAN SCOTLAND (SCOTTY) HARTMAN. There was no occupation or address or phone number or anything else. Only the name.

Bushong had described him as very old and very fat. Both descriptions fit, especially the very fat. Marty was not good at estimating a person's weight but this man had to weigh at least two hundred and fifty pounds. Maybe more, maybe as much as three hundred? Marty had no idea how old he was. Seventy? Seventy-five? Eighty? Who knew?

The important thing to keep in mind, Marty kept saying to himself, was that he was no less a terrorist, a blower-upper of Jaguars and all the rest, than was Henderson. Than was Bennett, the man the president of the United States had chosen to head the Central Intelligence Agency.

And here he was, sitting across the table from Marty and Senator Simmons in the intelligence committee's secure room in the Capitol. Henderson, of course, the man who would be George Washington, sat right there by him. He was looking harmless, almost collegiate, in his country tweeds again.

Marty had run nine laps around the Georgetown University track that morning, working on Simmons to show indignation toward these two men. The humidity was high and the combination of that and the strain of pleading with Simmons made it an unusually grinding, sweaty nine laps. They are toying with one of our democracy's most sacred institutions, he said as forcefully as he could while trying to breathe normally. But remember the water deal, Simmons said, neither perspiring nor breathing hard. The water aide was, in fact, jogging along with them on Simmons's other side. But this goes beyond that, Marty argued. Nothing goes beyond that, Simmons replied. But Simmons did more or less end up promising to make as good a show as he could in the short time he would be there in the committee's interview room.

Hartman's conduct, as it turned out, made it easier. His tone and words were snide and disrespectful toward Simmons from the very beginning. He turned a simple introductory Simmons question into a vile, intemperate, profane attack on Ollie North, one of Simmons's best friends in the Senate. The Hartman-Henderson strategy, strangely enough, appeared to be to piss everybody off.

Marty became concerned that matters might get out of hand. He'd pumped up Simmons so much he was afraid the senator might lose it. A big word fight with two former CIA men—leaked to the press, as everything was—at this particular point in time would not help his profile.

So, after a couple of heated Simmons-Hartman exchanges about loyalty, patriotism and blowing up cars, Marty moved to get Simmons out of there. He reminded the senator of a subcommittee hearing that was already under way on timber cutting in the national forests. Another aide sitting behind them chimed in with the additional reminder that a delegation from Roswell was in the senator's office, waiting to protest some liberal Democrat's bill to screw the prescription drug industry.

Then Hartman really did it. He got his fat, detestable self to his feet and said he was going back to West Virginia or some other place where the air and the people were cleaner.

At a full-volume scream, Simmons said, "I'll have you cited for contempt of the Senate!"

"Be my guest. I already have so much contempt it is only right that it be made official."

Marty knew this was it. One way or another, this was it. Either Simmons would go completely berzerk, ordering these two old men arrested and hanged by their necks until they are dead, or he would back off. There was no other place to go. All the way or no way.

Marty put a hand on the senator's arm. He hoped it said: Easy does it, sir. You are a United States senator, these two men are nothing. They're not worth losing it over. This situation is not worth losing it. Relax, sir.

Marty felt some tension leave the senator's arm. It was passing. Everything was going to be all right.

There were a few more nasty moments before Simmons finally left the room surrounded by his aides.

And then it was just him, Marty, and them, Henderson and Hartman.

Marty decided that he had to establish who was in charge now, who was calling the shots, who was terrorized and who was not. Hartman, looking to Marty more like a balloon than a man, was still standing, ready to take a walk—a waddle, actually—out of the room toward West Virginia.

Marty threatened subpoenas and other retaliation if Hartman and Henderson walked out. At first, Marty thought he'd made a mistake, as it set off Hartman to smirk about how he and Henderson spent their lives with threats of various kinds, young man. We don't scare. But then Hartman did lower himself back down into his chair and Marty scored one for his side—for himself, for the future voters of Connecticut and for Andrea and the children.

Hartman's tone remained uncivil and insulting for the most part, and he kept harping on Marty to explain why the committee was going after Josh Bennett.

And eventually Marty came close to losing his place and purpose. The question nagged and bothered him. Could Hartman tell that? Was that why he kept asking it? Could Hartman and Henderson, in addition to being terrorists, also have some supernatural mind-reading powers?

There, with the eyes of those two old spies on him, Marty's brain went through one of the most whamming and whacking experiences of its thirty-two-year-old life. Never before had he been called upon to make such a monumental decision.

On the one hand: All right, you two old bastards. Listen up. This whole thing is a goddamn fraud. Your friend Joshua Eugene Bennett is in no jeopardy. He will be confirmed as DCI. We are going through a little charade in government, a little square dance of deception. We are doing it so the people of New Mexico will get the water they so dearly need in order to survive and prosper. This has not one damned thing to do with the fitness of Joshua Eugene Bennett to be director of Central Intelligence. So, let's make a deal. You tell me what I want to know and I will help Simmons kick up exactly the right amount of fuss to make it possible for the Faucet to blackmail the White House into appointing his friend, and then the Faucet will give the people of New Mexico their water, Bennett will be confirmed and life in our democracy will go on undisturbed. I will then go home to contemplate and prepare for my wonderful future life with my wife, Andrea, and our three children in our lovely home on O Street,

Northwest. I will practice telling her about my life working in the field of the people, as she is doing. I will imagine how our children will ask questions about Jefferson, his vision from the rock at Harpers Ferry and his influence on us and our democracy. And then I will picture myself, late at night, dictating my feelings and opinions about my day into a Dictaphone so that long, long after I am gone they can be looked at by scholars. Maybe there will be a place for both Andrea's and my papers. The Andrea Bartlett and Martin V. Madigan Room of the Sterling Library at Yale might be such a place. We would, of course, endow it.

On the other hand: Not now, Andrea and you lovely children. I don't have time to think about you and the room in the library now. I am here now across the table from two old spooks—both old, one very fat. Here I am now, but I will not be here forever. What I do here may not be particularly great or worthy or honest, but it will lead to bigger and better things. Things that will be good for America. Someday I will be the senator who sets the new standards for service. There will be no more deals for votes in exchange for water or judgeships. The politics I practice will be politics for the public good. But for now, not all of the choices are mine. I have to deal with these two old bastards this afternoon. On with the Blue Heart story. On with real life.

Tell me the Blue Heart story, Mr. Henderson.

"The full story is in the files," Hartman said. "Why don't you simply get it from Bushong and read it."

Hartman was right. Marty had the file in front of him at the table, in fact. So he asked all of the obvious questions about the Czech and his pistol and received from Henderson all of the obvious lies and evasions in response. Each exchange was accompanied by a screw-you smile or crack from Hartman. Marty finally told the very large man that he was wasting his time if he thought he was going to provoke him.

Marty felt he held his own in the remaining back-and-forths and, with some gusto, even rattled off a phony warning about the active pursuit of the Jaguar bombing investigation. He could tell by Hartman's and Henderson's mildly amused looks that they, too, must believe the D.C. police couldn't find a monkey in a zoo—or however Bushong had put it.

Then Marty fell for what was clearly a trap. Hartman said something about missing their train back to West Virginia. Marty had read a non-headed Bushong memorandum on the table in front of him that summarized the activities of Hartman and Henderson, including the fact that they had made arrangements to drive to Washington that morning. And, without thinking, Marty blurted out, "You didn't come by train." That gave Hartman the perfect opportunity to make a speech about the Senate's being involved in the surveillance of private citizens and a lot of other crap.

He was caught. Marty had no choice but to ignore it and push on as best he could. He asked Henderson how well Bennett accounted for his expenses with the CIA.

Henderson answered with an absolute lie, followed by others that were even worse. Marty, by then, did not mind. Thank you, Mr. Henderson, he thought. You have just provided me with some ammunition for possible use in future encounters. It's called perjury.

Marty closed the files on the table and made a speech about people in the Central Intelligence Agency, past and present, who might think they are above the laws of the land, laws that include those against blowing up XJ6 Jaguars parked in front of fire hydrants. He promised Hartman and Henderson full and prompt investigation of and prosecution for any and all crimes they might commit in the name of trying to help their friend Joshua Bennett.

Hartman, as could be expected, responded with another savage, by now predictable attack on all the liars in the United States Senate.

Don't think I am confused about what you two old fools are up to! Marty wanted to yell at these two old fools. You are in the business of provocation. Make 'em mad, make 'em do something stupid and embarrassing.

Well, you're out of luck. I'm not going to do anything stupid.

Marty was glad afterward that he had not eaten all of the stuffed veal chop, baked new potatoes and asparagus tips that lay on the plate in front of him. He did not believe he could have done so without retching, without throwing up all over himself and several others present in that small dining room of the Metropolitan Club.

The occasion plus the words made for a retching evening.

"We have our differences and we have our different responsibilities and different functions," said Senator Maloney to the group of a hundred and twenty-five men and women in black tie and fancy dresses. "But it is on occasions such as this when we come together over a drink and a simple meal that we pause, ponder and remind ourselves of what we have in common.

"And that, of course, is our general and mutual commitment to maintaining the defense of our beloved country and the specific and mutual commitment to maintaining the superb intelligence force and apparatus that makes that defense possible and thus keeps our country free."

Senator Maloney, the chairman of the Senate Select Committee on Intelligence, then raised his glass of red wine, a 1987 Rhone. "Ladies and gentlemen, a toast."

Marty joined the others in standing and raising their glasses of wine.

Maloney said, "To Josh Bennett, the man chosen by our president to direct this superb intelligence force and apparatus!"

There was a chorus of "Hear, hear."

Then Senator Simmons rose from another of the twelve round tables in the room, which was decorated in the English country decor favored by men's clubs the world over. The Metropolitan, among the very last of the Washington clubs to accept women members, would never look any different.

After getting the group's attention with a couple of spoon taps to a glass, Simmons said, "We from the other side of the aisle also want to raise our voices and our glasses to our joint commitment to a sound defense and a vital intelligence service. We raise them as well to Joshua Bennett, the nominee for director of Central Intelligence, and to the constitutionally mandated advise-and-consent function of the United States Senate, which is now considering his nomination.

"To our commitment, to Mr. Bennett and to our constitutionally mandated process."

The people said "Hear, hear" again.

Marty had written those words for Simmons. But he hadn't wanted to have anything to do with any of this. The idea of the senator's participating in this dinner had seemed ridiculous, hypocritical, cynical, duplicitous and dishonest to Marty. A hearings-eve dinner seemed like a stupid idea to begin with, but for Simmons to cohost it was particularly stupid.

He had said to the senator, "It just doesn't seem right to toast a man while at the same time doing . . . well, what we are doing with his nomination in order to . . . well, make a deal over water."

"In this world, our world, Marty, what you see is seldom what you see," responded Senator Simmons, the second-ranking Republican in the Senate and the ranking minority member of the Senate Select Committee on Intelligence.

The dinner was on the verge of breaking up when a waiter told Marty he had a phone call.

It was Bushong on an open-line phone. He told Marty that Scotty Hartman was dead.

"I hope, I pray to all the gods, it was natural causes," Marty said. "Jesus, if you guys killed him . . . Jesus. I can see how you were upset about your car but Jesus, Russ."

"He died on his own," Bushong said. "We don't kill people. Not anymore. Not even for blowing up my car."

"He looked sick to me today, come to think of it. And he certainly acted a kind of sick . . ."

"We'll cover the funeral," Bushong said. "It'll bring them all out from under their rocks."

Marty wasn't exactly sure what that meant but he didn't care.

"Give my respects to the DCI-designate and all of his little helpers and keepers," Bushong said before hanging up.

Marty had trouble imagining Hartman dead. He could not see such a large person embalmed in a casket with flowers all around and organ music playing.

It was Henderson's fault, he would tell the senator. The strain of dealing with the subpoena and the interview session and Bennett's nomination was too much. That killed Hartman, sir. Henderson killed Hartman.

We didn't kill Hartman, Senator.

I didn't kill Hartman.

PART 3

CHARLIE AND MARTY

November

NINE

Charlie could never have found the room again if his life depended on it, and he was not completely sure it did not. He didn't realize the Senate of the United States had such a maze of private and unknown places down narrow hallways, around corners and behind unmarked doors. It was a large office that seemed to belong to no one; it had furniture, but no papers on the desk, nothing but nondescript reference books in a small bookshelf, no photographs or other personal items anywhere. There wasn't even an umbrella or a forgotten raincoat or slicker on the coatrack. It reminded him of some Agency safe houses and offices that he'd passed through in his day.

Josh was there with three of his well-combed and well-polished young suits, men in their early thirties who looked exactly like what they were—employees of the Central Intelligence Agency. They were probably born looking the way they did. Charlie could never make some of the people in charge understand that real CIA officers shouldn't go around looking like movie-version CIA officers.

But that was not the issue here this morning. Charlie had come to the Capitol unofficially to help Josh but officially because he was under subpoena, although it was still not clear to him whether he would actually be called to testify. And, having decided not to get another lawyer to replace Scotty, he was flying solo.

"Anything new I should know, Charlie?" Josh said. He had motioned for Charlie to join him over in a corner, out of hearing of the suits.

"Nope." They had not had a serious conversation about much of anything since that evening at DeCarlo's. "We still don't know exactly what's going on. I am so sorry about that, Josh."

"Our people say there may be less to it than meets the eye," Josh said. "I may be a secondary target—maybe even a feint target."

"Does that make sense, Josh? Why can't they find out for sure?"

"We can use a satellite to read the goddamn watermark on a piece of toilet paper on the way up the president of Iran but we can't find out why our own Congress does what it does," Josh said.

Several smart responses came to Charlie's mind. Such as, how in the hell can you find out why people who don't know themselves why they are doing something are doing something? Or, if it was only toilet paper that was on its way up the members of the United States Senate then . . .

But that was not the issue here this morning.

Marty was in a similar office down a similar hall around similar corners and behind similar unmarked doors. He was there alone—absolutely alone—with Senator Simmons. There wasn't a single water aide or grazing aide present.

Simmons was thumbing through a written statement Marty had just handed him. "What am I saying?" he asked Marty.

"You are praising the process whereby the president nominates and the Senate confirms. You are noting the long service the nominee has given to the people and the government of the United States. You are looking forward to hearing from him and others about his plans and visions for the future of the intelligence community in this ever changing post–Cold War world."

"Good. Is the rest in process?"

"Yes. We're aiming for this afternoon."

"Grover's got to believe it."

"He will."

"Then the White House has got to believe it. Did you see the clips this morning on the Park Service?"

The Park Service? "No, sir."

"They may have to close down a few national parks. We have more than few in New Mexico. It's always something. If it's not our military bases or our water, it's our parks. Here we go again."

Here we go again, thought Marty. Let's see: There's a national park down a canyon outside Taos that will surely be shut and abandoned unless a powerful Senate committee chairman intercedes. That chairman wants Simmons to get the son of his college roommate appointed CIA station chief in Paris . . .

Andrea, are we sure we want to be senators? Even a different, perfect kind of senator?

"Remember C-Span," one of the secretaries in the office had warned the night before. "Don't fall asleep or look bored or pick your nose or shoot the finger or anything like that."

Marty did not have to be reminded about C-Span. His designated place in the hearing room was right behind Simmons in a chair against the wall. That meant that he would be in the background of the television shot whenever Simmons was speaking. And that was the reason he wore his best Republican everything—a dark blue suit, light blue shirt, solid dark wine tie. He also made damned sure his socks matched and that they were calf length with firm elastic at the top so they wouldn't fall down. There were those who believed that nothing said more about a man than some bare skin on a crossed leg. Marty wouldn't go that far but he did believe there was something vaguely important about making sure no bare leg of his would show on national television.

Charlie had no designated seating position. The committee subpoena said only that he was to be present and available in case the committee decided to call him as a formal public witness. So he simply moved into the hearing room on the second floor of the Russell Office Building with the rest of the spectators. He took a seat on a row fairly far back. There were seats for about one hundred or so. Most of them were occupied. Who are these people? Charlie wondered. Who goes to the confirmation hearings of the nominee for director of Central Intelligence? A lot of old people, for one thing, he noticed. Is it because they have nothing else to do? Are they old Agency people? Spy buffs? Intelligence officers from other countries—including Russia? And a lot of young people were there too. Charlie figured they were mostly graduate students writing papers or dissertations about the Senate confirmation process or collecting and using intelligence in the post–Cold War world or something else that nobody much cared about except their professors. He thought of all the money these kids must be costing their parents. How can normal people afford to send their kids to college anymore?

There was the sound of a gavel banging. Seven senators—six men and one woman—were sitting up at the committee table. Josh Bennett was in front and below them, facing them from behind a small witness table. The junior and senior senators from his home state of Massachusetts sat on either side of him.

"The committee will be in order," said the man responsible for the banging, Senator Jake Maloney, Democrat, of Maine, the chairman of the Senate Intelligence Committee.

Early on Marty had asked Simmons the obvious question:

Why doesn't Grover the Faucet simply go through Maloney, a fellow Democrat and a powerful committee chairman, to put the proper scare into the White House about the Bennett nomination? Simmons had replied that he had no idea. He said such mysteries and unanswered questions were part of what made serving in the United States Senate so fascinating. Marty, at that particular moment, might have used another word than "fascinating."

Maloney welcomed Joshua Eugene Bennett to his confirmation hearings and told him that it would be a while before they actually got around to hearing from him. First, there would be introducing statements by his two home-state senators, the two distinguished gentlemen there at the table with him. Then the seven senators up at the other table—the distinguished members of the committee—had opening statements. Then Bennett, the nominee, would be sworn as a witness and listened to.

Charlie had attended only a few congressional hearings. Mary Jane had taken to watching some of them on C-Span when there was something really important happening. Through the years he had watched the big ones, such as the Iran-Contra, the Watergate and Nixon impeachment hearings and, most important, the Church Committee hearings that so devastated the Agency and several of his own friends—and enemies—who worked there with him. And, of course, he had sat right there in embarrassed amazement with the rest of the country during the Anita Hill–Clarence Thomas affair. But that was about it for his own recent exposure.

It was the conduct of the senators during Hill-Thomas that had left the most lasting impression. He was struck by how all of them had seemed to think it was about themselves, not about Anita Hill or Clarence Thomas or sexual harassment or the Supreme Court of the United States or truth or consequences. It was about me, the senator now speaking. And there was that sticky politeness between them that cast an additional film of unreality and phoniness over all that was said and done. Charlie, after listening only a few minutes to this set of senators, could tell that nothing had changed. All senators are created to perform equally.

Marty, after five of the senators had spoken, wondered how he would handle himself at hearings like this when he became a senator. Maybe he would not make any statements, not even ask any questions. Sometimes he would come and listen, but he would never talk. Never ever talk. These hearings are all such exercises in self-importance, he thought. And then he quickly scolded himself for thinking something that was not only unfair but untrue. These people really are important. There are only one hundred United States senators. They come right after the president and the vice president and the chief justice of the Supreme Court, the chairman of the Federal Reserve—and maybe a computer billionaire or two and a few movie stars, some television people and possibly a few pro athletes—as the truly most important people in the United States of America. These senators, including the one who just read the words I wrote for him, are in fact important. So why not let them talk on and on, let them preen and prance like racehorses, let aides and interns pick up their clips and jog with them and do whatever else is needed for and by them. Important people have the right to act important. Even if it's boring and embarrassing sometimes to be present when they do.

Maloney and Simmons were the only senators still present when Maloney asked Josh Bennett to stand and raise his right hand. The others, per custom, had come, read their opening statements and scurried off to attend to more important matters. Senators always had more important things to do than attend hearings, unless they were the presiding chairman or ranking minority member or, more important, the hearings were the subject of special public and press attention.

"Do you swear that the testimony you will give before this Senate Select Committee on Intelligence will be the truth, the whole truth and nothing but the truth, so help you God?" said Maloney.

"I do," said Bennett.

"You may be seated," Maloney said. "Mr. Bennett, I understand you have an opening statement."

"That is true, Senator."

"You may read it, sir."

Bennett sat down, cleared his throat, put on a pair of half-lens reading glasses and began: "Mr. Chairman, Mr. Vice Chairman—"

"Excuse me, Mr. Bennett," Maloney interrupted. He was listening to Simmons say something to him in a very audible whisper. "I've got to run back and see about one of our parks."

"Parks?"

"I think they're going to try to close down one of mine."

"They better keep their hands off of ours in Maine."

"They wouldn't dare touch any of yours."

"They closed one of our navy bases."

"That's different."

"How much time do you need?"

"About ten minutes."

"I'll announce a five-minute break and then we'll let her slide."

"Thank you, Mr. Chairman."

Simmons's aide who had handed the park-alert note to Marty to hand to Simmons was waiting just out the rear door of the meeting room. Simmons disappeared with him as Maloney announced the recess.

This is ridiculous! screamed Marty to himself. We're here to consider the nomination of the person who will be in charge of the most powerful and important intelligence service on the face of earth. And here he goes, running like a scared rabbit after some little park outside Taos.

It was only then that he saw Charles Henderson out there in the audience. The old spy-bomber-terrorist-bastard was standing up now as if to go out into the hallway for some air. Marty went around the end of the senators' table, down to the floor and through the public doorway to the hallway. He made for Charlie, who was leaning against a wall.

"Mr. Henderson," said Marty, offering no other word or gesture of greeting. "Blown up any cars since I saw you last?"

"Unfairly harassed any other qualified nominees for high

office since I saw *you* last?" Charlie replied without a blink or a second's hesitation.

Gotcha, boy, thought Charlie.

Not bad for an old man, thought Marty.

"I'll be glad to have somebody blow up your car, Mr. Madigan, if that's what you want," said Charlie, moving to press his advantage. "Are you in it for the insurance money or what?"

Marty decided that this was a game he should not be playing with this old man. Age sometimes does have its advantages, and it was clear this was one of those times. How many games of wits and whatever had this man Henderson played in his life? How many times had he had to think fast on his feet, as he'd just done? How many times had his life been hanging in the balance? Marty remembered a famous Notre Dame football coach who said there's only one thing worse than not showing up for the game and that is showing up with only ten players. In this game, Marty thought, he would always only have ten players to Henderson's eleven.

"I was sorry to hear about Hartman," Marty said.

Charlie knew this young man was not sorry at all about Scotty. But he said nothing.

Marty figured why not fire one small parting shot just to show there's still life on the other side. "I understand there are still several of you involved now in trying to protect Mr. Bennett from his past."

"Are those your people watching us up there in West Virginia at funerals and other places or are they Bushong's?" Charlie shot back. "We thought about following your watching rats back to their holes but decided we didn't care. Rats tend to all look alike from the rear."

End of the recess, end of a small Charlie-Marty firefight.

Josh Bennett read his entire statement. It took him twenty-one minutes. He went through the changes in the world in the last ten years—the collapse of Communism in Eastern Europe and then in the Soviet Union, the dissolution of the Soviet Union, Yugoslavia and Czechoslovakia, the Persian Gulf War, the North Korean nuclear threat and the rise of Muslim fundamentalism. He spoke to growing fears about nuclear proliferation and terrorism, to the growing need for intelligence about agriculture, weather and economics. He rattled off a list of CIA triumphs that was so well scrubbed that it was difficult to understand what in the hell he was talking about. He spoke of technological breakthroughs that had already been made and the many unknown ones still to come. He praised the many thousands of silent heroes in the intelligence service who had labored for their country—sometimes at great risk to their own personal safety. He took the opportunity to thank the families of those intelligence officers, who had made their own sacrifices for their country. He finished with a brief statement about his own experience and with a pledge—if confirmed—to carry on the great traditions and performances of the greatest intelligence service in the world.

Charlie could have done without much of the first part but loved the last about the silent heroes. Overall he thought it was about eleven minutes too long, and he wished Josh was a better and more dynamic public speaker. His voice was pitched too high and he was saddled with a Massachusetts accent that made him sound like a guy giving the rush-hour traffic report from a helicopter flying above Boston. Charlie agreed with what Reynolds had said the other night in the back of the bread truck: Josh is admittedly a bit on the ordinary side—certainly not flashy, to say the least. But so what? He had been superb in the field and tough, fair and loyal as a supervisor. The Agency could do with some quiet, ordinary leadership for a while. Besides, he's a good man and he's my friend.

Marty thought Bennett's statement was absolutely brilliant. Not since he heard Senator Moynihan speak last year at a Council on Foreign Relations dinner in New York City had he heard such a brilliant summary of what was going on in the new world. Whether Bennett wrote it himself or not—and he probably didn't—it showed that somebody close to him at the Agency had a firm grip on reality and had the ability to make sense out of it.

Let's hear it for the spies of America! thought Charlie.

I guess it's good this anti-Bennett thing is not for real, thought Marty.

I wonder if they had a bug in Juan's garage the other night? thought Charlie.

But let's not forget they blew up Bushong's Jag, thought Marty.

Why would Josh even want the goddamn job, thought Charlie.

He did cheat on his expense reports, too, thought Marty.

Why don't those other bastards want him to have it? thought Charlie.

What are they hiding about Berlin? thought Marty.

Did Carla Avery talk to them? thought Charlie.

I wonder if Andrea is watching this on C-Span, thought Marty.

Maybe Mary Jane will see me in a background camera shot, thought Charlie.

It was after Charlie had walked across the street from the Russell Building to a park bench under some trees and had a solitary and wonderful lunch of two street-vendor hot dogs with dollops of chili, chopped onions, grated cheese and mustard. It was after Maloney had reconvened the afternoon session and then immediately recessed it while he and the other two senators present—neither was Simmons—went to the floor to vote. It was after Maloney had come back from voting and begun his questioning of Josh about subjects that seemed incredibly obscure and irrelevant. It was after Charlie had fought back dozing off for more than an hour.

Half-awake, he felt the warmth of a body slipping into the seat next to his. Then he felt the soft blow of an elbow into his right arm.

It was Jay Buckner, the invisible man of action turned seller of real estate.

Jay moved his eyes to his right. Please come with me, Charlie.

Charlie followed Jay from a distance to a spot outside in the same park where he had had his solitary and wonderful lunch. He joined Jay on another bench.

"I got into the place back of the fisheries last night," Jay said. "All that's happening is a lot of male fish having it off with a lot of female fish."

Charlie, man of the world of intelligence and espionage, suddenly realized a serious gap in his knowledge. He had lived to the age of sixty-eight and did not know how fish had it off. Do they have at their disposal the same kind of equipment for that sort of thing that animals and humans have?

He chose not to ask Jay that question. Instead, he said, "There's got to be more to it than that."

"They are obviously taking some kind of oil out of the pregnant female fish, who, by the way, look different from the males. The males are light, the females are dark."

"We're talking mixed marriage here?"

"I have no idea what we're talking, Charlie."

"What do they do with the oil?"

"Keep in mind that nobody was there doing anything when I was there about two A.M. The only nonfish present were three armed watchmen who did not know I was there and never will. The others were presumably all snug in their off-duty beds somewhere. I was looking at everything with an ultraviolet light. I saw the fish and I read some daily activity books and looked at some test tubes and beakers and at the labels on them and everything else I could find. That's it. So what do they do with the oil? As best I could see, they put it into small—one-inch-tall—metal jars and seal the lids. I brought one of them with me." He patted his right suitcoat pocket. "What should I do with it?"

"Is there oil in it?"

"You got it."

"Won't they miss it?"

"If they didn't notice Ames they won't notice one little jar of fish oil is missing."

"Keep it in a safe place."

Jay patted his suitcoat pocket again.

"Anything else?

"Nothing. What did you mean when you said you thought there might be something there that could help Josh?"

"It was just a hunch," Charlie said.

"How's he doing in there?" Jay said, pointing back toward the Russell Building.

"It's a tie. Everybody is boring everybody. Josh is both a borer and a bored."

Charlie had two further questions for Jay: Is it possible Bushong or somebody had a wire in Juan's garage? Is it possible Carla Avery is cooperating with Madigan and company? Jay said he had no idea about number one. On number two he said, "Sure. She hates you and me and Josh and everybody else like us. What does she know that could hurt Josh?"

"Probably nothing," Charlie said. Another day, another lie.

Charlie had come down to Washington on the train. Jay said he was welcome to ride back with him at the end of the day. Terrific, said Charlie.

On their way back into the Russell Office Building Charlie stopped at a pay phone to call Harpers Ferry and leave a message on the answering machine of Rosebud Sam's Antique Toys.

. . .

Marty was willing to take crap and commotion from a United States senator in the line of duty and for the further-ance of the American democracy and the Republican Party. But this senatorial privilege was not transferable. He would never under any circumstances take even the whiff of same from a senator's assistant, aide or whatever. Since acting as if they were in fact the senator for whom they worked was the stock-in-trade of most of them, this policy often led to tense meetings like the two he had after the hearings adjourned that afternoon.

The first was with Jack Allen, the chief majority coun-sel of the Senate Intelligence Committee. He was Marty's counterpart on the other side of the aisle, which made him his colleague in the search for truth in the furtherance of bi-partisan oversight of the gathering and distributing of intelli-gence in the government of the United States. Allen, a native of Camden, Maine, who had worked for a while as a trial lawyer in the Justice Department's criminal division, was al-most the same age as Marty and as far as Marty could tell was almost the same in every other way except in his political be-liefs. Allen was obsessively interested in a political career, probably in one that led to his becoming a United States senator. He was for the moment most interested in making sure nothing happened in the world of American intelligence that reflected badly on his mentor, Senator Maloney, on him-self or on the Democratic party. Allen was the one who had finally gotten Maloney and the president to withdraw the earlier nomination of that jerk Joe Phillip Jackson as DCI. Marty, too, had made his contributions to that effort by relaying every bit of bad news or speculation or possibility to Allen so he could scare the senator into scaring the White House.

It was to do a similar bit of duty on Bennett that he had requested a private meeting with Allen, a tall guy who let his dark blond hair grow like an unclipped bush. His windowless "secure" office, where they were meeting, was a mess of stacked papers and books, the result of Allen's paranoid security policy that kept secretaries and clerks from ever entering to file or tidy up.

Marty laid out in general terms Senator Simmons's "growing concern" about Bennett's track record with money and telling the truth about Berlin.

"You're going after Bennett?" Allen said, throwing his large hands and arms into the air in a gesture of utter disbelief. "Give me a break, please. This guy is as good and clean as they come. There are no marks of Ames or anything else on him. This must be a feint of some kind. Nobody in their right mind could be serious about going after Bennett."

"Simmons is in his right mind and he is serious," Marty replied with all the sincerity he could muster.

"I would prefer to put on hold for now any discussion about the mind of Lank Simmons," Allen said.

"When it comes to intelligence and integrity, he could wipe the floor with Maloney any day, any time, any place."

"People like us don't have to talk this way to each other, Marty."

"People like us are in charge of how we talk, Jack. We can talk any damned way we wish."

"Is Simmons going to raise this unsubstantiated dirt and slander with Bennett in open session on live C-Span tomorrow?" Allen asked.

"He's thinking about it."

"That would be unconscionable."

"I'm sorry."

"No, you're not. 'Sorry' is a word we do not have to ever use, Marty. Are you hunting for a deal of some kind? What's going on?"

"Nothing's going on yet. I just didn't want you and your senator to get blindsided if something does eventually go on, that's all."

"You can tell your senator for me . . ."

"Need I remind you that I do not deliver messages to my senator from staff."

The second meeting was with and in the office of the chief of staff of the Senate Natural Resources Subcommittee of the Commerce Committee. He was Gregory Robertson, Grover the Faucet's top water man, who had been a lawyer in private practice in Silsbee, Texas, and chairman of the Texas State Democratic Committee before coming to Washington. It was often said around the Senate that his knowledge of water went no further than knowing when to say "when" to a bartender pouring water into a glass of bourbon and ice.

"The White House won't budge until they hear the sound of Bennett's balls being crushed in my big right hand here," said Gregory, holding that very right hand up to show Marty he really did have one. "And neither will we."

"You'll hear it."

"When?"

"If you'll stop talking for a minute you can hear it now."

Robertson got the joke but he clearly did not like being told to stop talking. So he didn't.

"Grover has to go to the White House with the smell of blood right there in his hand," said Robertson, holding up his right hand again.

Marty fought off the visual image of what he was supposed to imagine was bleeding in Grover's right hand.

"So sniff," Marty said, sniffing.

"Sniff?"

"That's right."

Robertson sniffed and said, "I don't pick up a whiff of anything but sweet Republican baby puke."

"That's because you're only sniffing through your left nostril." Not a bad line, thought Marty, quite proud of himself.

Robertson showed no sign of appreciation. "You tell your senator that my senator needs a smoking gun—a pubic-hair-on-a-Coca-Cola-can kind of thing, if you know what I mean, Madigan. Something that says we mean business in a way that requires no explanation—no sniffing."

"This conversation is between us," Marty said. "I don't like being told to deliver messages."

"That is all we do, Madigan. That is all we are— messenger boys. We do not exist as real people. Not while we're doing these jobs, doing the kind of shit we are doing right at this moment. Our time may eventually come, in its own way for each of us, but this ain't it."

"Tell your senator that my senator is prepared to go public with the charge that Joshua Bennett is a thief and a liar. His thievery has to do with real money and it has a history that begins in childhood and continues to his career in the Central Intelligence Agency. His lying includes an episode that resulted in the near death of a colleague in a confrontation with Communists."

"Now we're talking," Robertson said, putting his right hand up in the air again and squeezing his fingers together and down on something he seemed to be holding in the palm of his hand.

Marty wanted out of there.

Robertson, squeezing his hand together once more, put his left index finger to his forehead and said, "Who was it said, 'When you got 'em here, you got 'em there?' "

"Thomas Jefferson."

TEN

Charlie had done exactly what Sam had told him to do. He had come at precisely seven-thirty P.M. to the back door of the store, knocked twice, counted to three, knocked once, counted to two and knocked three times. There are burglars, holdup men, antique toy thieves and other threats to a peaceful society even here in the Panhandle of West Virginia, Sam had explained.

"Look what I just got," Sam said once Charlie was inside the Inner Sanctum.

There in the middle of the room was a large wooden

crate. The lid was off and around it on the floor were numerous toy airplanes. All were painted in the colors of various U.S. airlines, mostly those that no longer existed—Braniff, Bowen, Eastern, Frontier, Northeast, Mohawk, Capitol, Allegheny, Trans Texas. Some of the planes were made of tin, others of cast iron or wood. They were in several sizes and models but all were propeller planes.

"I bought this whole collection from the estate of a dentist in North Carolina," Sam said, sitting down on a small milking stool next to the box and the planes. Charlie sat in a chair directly across from him. "He started collecting these things when he was a kid. He died last year and finally his widow agreed to part with the collection. They are beautiful, aren't they, Charlie?"

Beautiful? That was not the exact word Charlie would have used. They were certainly fun to look at. And they certainly triggered many nostalgic memories of past flights and past visits to airports. But beautiful? Not really. The idea of grown-ups collecting antique toys had come slowly to Charlie. He was there in a minor way with his few milk trucks, but he could not imagine going as far as Sam, that dead dentist in North Carolina and the thousands of other old men around the world who went nuts over the sight and feel of old cast-iron fire trucks or other toys.

"What does something like that go for?" Charlie asked. At that moment Sam was holding a model of what looked to Charlie to be a seaplane in the colors of Pan Am.

"I paid about five hundred for it. I'll put out there on the shelf asking double that."

One thousand dollars for a toy seaplane?

"That *was* you I saw on the Leetown Road the other morning," Charlie said after a while. By then all the airplanes were out of the box, out of their old newspaper wrappings and arranged on the floor around Sam as if they were on an airplane-museum tarmac somewhere off an interstate in Iowa or Florida. It reminded Charlie of a scene from *Gulliver's Travels.* The giant surrounded by a midget world.

"I will not talk about it, Charlie," Sam said. "It's nothing personal, it's professional. I can't."

"Why did you deny it was you I saw?"

"No talking about that, Charlie. None at all, sorry."

"You're still working for the Agency, aren't you?"

"Charlie, please . . ."

"That early-retirement story and this shop are all cover, aren't they? They must have really wanted you out here. The kind of money they must have tied up in these toys has got to be something. This ain't no Laundromat, Sam. I remember a Laundromat we ran as a cover for a guy off a side street near Holland Park in London. A lot of the workers at the Russian embassy did their clothes in the place. But this is in another league than that. You really held them up, Sam."

"Talk all you like . . ."

"There's something going on back up there behind the fisheries and you are in charge of it—involved in a big way, at least, if not in charge. Josh himself in this very room said the project was rather stupid, strange—silly. I don't remember exactly what he said. Stupid or strange or silly. But whatever, there you are, Sam. You're doing something that even the new DCI-designate thinks is either stupid or strange."

Charlie stopped to see if Sam would say anything. Sam

didn't. He was making a big thing of not saying anything, in fact. He held a model of a DC-3 in his right hand as if he were about to throw it into the sky and see if it could fly. It was painted in the blue-and-white color scheme of the old Southern Airways, which became a part of Republic, which later merged with Northwest.

"I know about the fish oil, Sam," Charlie said, watching Sam carefully for some reaction. "I know you're taking oil out of dark female fish who have had sex with and have been impregnated by light male fish. How do fish do that kind of thing, Sam? That's what I really want to know."

"No answers, Charlie." There was a slight change in the coloring in Sam's face up around the hairline. It was enough to let Charlie know Sam was stunned to learn what Charlie knew about what was going on in that fish lab.

Charlie said, "It cannot be a violation of the law of the land to tell me and the whole world, for that matter, how fish screw."

Sam shook his head, set the Southern plane down and picked up a very small cast-iron plane painted in Allegheny colors.

"I have a hunch you're doing something that could help Josh," Charlie said.

That did it. Sam set the Allegheny plane down on the floor and said, "I assure you, Charlie, that is not so. Believe me, if I thought for one minute . . . never mind."

It was now time for Charlie to take some chances, to take some flights into the unknown.

"Sam, allow me to think out loud with you for a few minutes, please."

"I'm already late for dinner."

"So am I. So let's try to figure this thing out as quickly as we can so we can both go to our respective homes and eat our respective suppers. Let's say you are me trying to figure out why the Agency would have you involved in anything having to do with oil from pregnant fish. You are not a scientist, a biologist, a doctor. You have no special knowledge or expertise of any kind in any of the science and technology areas. One would like to hope that not even nervousness over how to stay in business in the new post–Cold War, post-Ames world would cause Langley to go that crazy, to suddenly declare people experts in areas completely foreign to them. So there's got to be a connection between that fish oil and your area of expertise. And your area of expertise, of course, is interrogation. Asking people questions. You were—are—the very best. A legend within legends. You could get a deaf-mute to talk—wasn't that the line about you? So what in the hell is the connection between fish oil and asking people questions? Obviously you don't need it to ask the questions. Wouldn't you say that was obvious, Sam?"

"I'm hungry, Charlie."

"I'm getting warm, aren't I?"

"I'm hungry . . ."

"So if it doesn't have to do with the questions it must have something to do with the answers."

Charlie also had been really good in his own way at getting answers when there weren't any. He did it by noticing twitches and glances and by sniff and intuition. That training and experience caused him to know now with absolute certainty that he had just scored a direct hit on Sam Holt.

But it wasn't enough. The hard part was still to come.

"Well, then," he continued, "if it has to do with the answers, then it must mean there is something in that oil from that particular pregnant dark fish that affects the person being asked the question. Are we, the United States of America, on the development trail of a new and exotic truth serum? Something so exotic and wonderful that the top interrogator for the Central Intelligence Agency has been elaborately covered to operate at a supersecret facility over a hill in that wild and wonderful place called West Virginia?"

He waited again for Sam Holt to speak.

"It's neither exotic nor wonderful," Sam spoke. "That's all I will say."

"Sam, please!"

"Trust me, Charlie. There is nothing in this that would help Josh's confirmation problem."

"If it makes people tell the truth, it might."

Charlie knew that Sam knew he had gone too far already. He was the master interrogator. He had told Charlie and anyone else in the Agency who would listen that there was only one big rule of interrogation. Short of blackmail, straight payoff and torture—physical or psychological or chemical—there was no way to get people to talk against their will. The rule—the secret, the procedure—is to grease the way for the person to decide on his or her own to talk. So, by that logic, Sam had said too much already, and Charlie knew he'd done so because he'd decided to. Now all that remained to be found out was what his decision would be about the rest of the story.

Sam picked up a three-foot-long model of an Eastern Airlines four-engine Constellation, a plane Charlie had flown to Europe and elsewhere in the world in the late fifties and early sixties more times than he cared to remember.

"I was on one of those—it was a BOAC, I think—when it lost two of its engines just after we left Shannon," he said to Sam. "Fortunately we had a good pilot and a good plane and we had a happy ending."

"Let's go outside, Charlie," Sam said.

They put on their coats and Charlie followed Sam out the back door into the darkness. It was a typical deep autumn evening. Cool enough for a sweater and a light jacket and maybe a pair of gloves. There was a bright moon. Without really thinking about it, Charlie glanced around to see if there were any suspicious parked cars around. He had not seen any earlier when he arrived. He still didn't.

It was clear to Charlie that this walk was not to a destination. It was only to be outside, to be away from four walls, a roof and a floor. They fell into a slow amble down Washington Street toward the main business section of Harpers Ferry. It was downhill. There were a few lights ahead from restaurants and a few small specialty shops and gift shops that remained open after dark.

"The other side knows about our meeting in Juan's garage," Charlie said as they walked.

"That's no surprise," Sam said. "That's why we're out here on the street in the cold now. I don't know how or why but it's possible somebody's got a little something with ears in my place."

Charlie did not have to be told that. Now, Sam, talk, please.

Sam let only a few more steps and seconds pass before he spoke. "You got it, Charlie. I'm still on the string, I'm here on assignment. I don't know how you found out about the fish and the oil but you had that mostly right, too. You're as good as everyone always said you were. The fish and the oil didn't start as ours. Some old KGB scientist bought his way into a plush new post–Cold War identity and life with a little jar of oil and that special formula for making some more. He said it was only a few experiments away from being the magic stuff we people who ask questions for a living have wet dreams about. The ultimate flutter, the ultimate grease job. You give it to someone without their knowing they got it. And then without realizing what they are doing, they sit there and answer truthfully all questions asked. There are no side-effects or after-effects. No needles, no coercion of any kind. You ask, they answer. No mess, no bother. When it's over the person doesn't really know what happened except that for some unexplained reason he told all and feels better for having done so."

They were still ambling along, two old friends out for a early-evening stroll in the deep autumn moonlight. They passed a coffeehouse that was brimming with people and the magnificent odor of espresso and cappuccino. Charlie didn't want to stop Sam's stream of talk but he felt he had to say something. So he said, "Jesus, Sam."

"Jesus and all of the disciples, as they used to say in my neighborhood. And then some. You don't even have to be in our business to see the potential of such a thing. Not only in crime and court matters but all kinds of things."

Charlie said, "All of those Sunday-morning television interviewers would kill for it, for one thing . . ."

"So would every teacher . . ."

"And priest . . ."

"And wife . . ."

"And husband . . ."

"And parent."

Jesus and all of the disciples is definitely right, Charlie thought to himself.

That thought was followed by another. "How is it administered?"

"It's still just in the oil-only stage," Sam said. "And the only way it seems to work is if it's administered down through the scalp into the brain."

"So the Agency's going to train everybody to be barbers? It doesn't sound terribly practical to me."

"It's not and it may never be. Josh thinks it's too tricky and dangerous to continue. Stupid, strange and silly—weren't they the words he used with you? He said to me the other day when he was up here that he was also not sure it remained in the public interest to create something so invasive of personal privacy. The potential for evil is more than that for good. And he's probably right. So why not stop it now before it's too late? was his question, which, if and when he's confirmed as DCI, I'm sure he will answer. Good-bye, Rosebud Sam's Antiques. Would you like to buy some antique toy and model airliners, sir?"

"Besides the store cover, you must have some seriously mixed feelings about closing down the fish."

"I do. I would like to see it a little bit further along, just to know if it really would work."

They walked and talked for another twenty minutes before saying good night back at the shop.

"How do fish screw, Sam?" was Charlie's final question.

"With a smooth grace and elegance—just like they swim" was Sam's answer.

Senator Simmons wore black tie as a cover for the evening. His little black-tie lie, as he called it. He would be attending seven separate events—four dinners and three receptions. None were black tie but the fact that he was wearing a tuxedo would clearly suggest to those at all seven that the senator, bless his busy, much-in-demand heart, had come to their event on his way to an important affair at the F Street Club, an embassy or possibly even at the White House itself. Simmons had found it to be a most effective way to create the proper atmosphere for getting in and out of places in a hurry.

Spending the evening event-hopping with the senator was offered to Marty as the only way available for the two of them to get ready for tomorrow. Marty would not have to wear black tie himself. At most of the stops he wouldn't even have to get out of the five-year-old Ford station wagon the senator, as usual, drove himself.

On the ride between a reception in the Longworth House Office Building for a retiring House member from Arizona to another at the Capital Hyatt on New Jersey Avenue for a former House member who had just changed Washington law firms, Marty told the senator about his meeting with Jack Allen, the intelligence committee's majority counsel.

"The word is now out that you may go after Bennett tomorrow."

"I know. Maloney called a few minutes ago. He would like to see me for breakfast in the morning. He suggested that possibly you and Jack Allen might join us."

That was good news to Marty. There was no telling what Simmons might say or do on his own. The thought also brought a silent vow from Marty to make damned sure that he never became as dependent on his Senate staff as Simmons was on him.

"Let's talk about what we say at that breakfast," said Simmons.

"The first thing we say is that you are serious. You are truly concerned about putting a thief and a liar into the top intelligence position of the United States."

"I am not prepared to say thief and liar."

"What about 'trimmer of the truth in a financial as well as the regular way'?"

The senator, wheeling the car up into the front of the Hyatt, did not react. Marty was not sure he had been heard.

On the ride from the Hyatt downtown to the Willard for a dinner honoring the incoming president of the American Processed Food Association, a former agriculture secretary in the Bush administration, Marty reported on his conversation with Robertson, the Faucet's chief water man.

"I think he thinks we have enough to do the trick," Marty said.

"Right again," said the senator. "Another call I got this afternoon was from Senator Grover. He said he could already hear the flow of fresh water through the parched fields of northern New Mexico. He said he planned to apply some squeeze at this next dinner, in fact. He said he planned to see and talk to Markel—you know, the White House guy."

"What's he going to say?"

In a phony, exaggerated Texas accent, Simmons said, "'I'm a-hearin' some bad, bad thangs about what some erful Republican is 'bout ta do to that Bennett spy fella. I may be in a perfect position to kill it deader 'na run-over coyotee if I knew I could tell my friend in El Paso something good and golden about his future as a judge.' Something along those lines."

Something along those lines.

"Grover gave me the wink and nod that he had delivered the message to Markel," said Simmons twenty minutes later as they walked from the Willard across Fourteenth Street to the J. W. Marriott Hotel to a dinner welcoming to Washington the new administrator of the Federal Aviation Administration, a Democrat, of course, but one with a New Mexico connection of sorts from having been stationed briefly at Kirtland Air Force Base in Albuquerque in the seventies.

"So the die is cast now," Marty said as they entered the revolving door at the Marriott. He was sure Simmons had not heard him. But this time it really didn't matter.

A few minutes later on the way back to the Willard and

to their car—a doorman, recognizing the senator from many similar drive-ups in the past, had said it was all right to leave it right there in front—Simmons reminded Marty of the mission.

"Think water, Marty. Water, cool and clear. Remember all of those old cowboy songs about water—cool, clear water. This is about water. This is not about Bennett. What is his first name? Abraham? I can't ever seem to remember it."

"Josh. As in Joshua."

"I knew it was something like that. Josh as in Joshua. That is a good way to remember it."

Marty chose to disregard the possibilty that Simmons was suggesting that all Jewish names sound alike. He knew Simmons was more sensitive than that.

On the way from the Willard up and around six blocks or so to the Motion Picture Association of America offices at Sixteenth and I, for a buffet supper and the showing of the movie *A River Runs Through It* in its plush screening room in honor of the cardiac rehabilitation unit at Georgetown Hospital, Marty found himself saying something he had not intended to say. At least not so soon and so directly.

"It may be that we—you—are more serious about this than we—you—may have imagined when it started," he said.

"I'm always serious. That's why I am where I am today."

Where are you today, Senator? Dressed in your little black-tie lie, you are driving your own old car because you're afraid some reporter will catch you being chauffeured on an evening of Washington groveling and ass-kissing. I really am going to be a different kind of senator.

"I mean about Joshua Bennett. Maybe he really shouldn't be DCI."

They were already parked in the MPAA parking garage. The comment drew no response from Simmons. Marty assumed he had not been heard.

On the way from the MPAA dinner to the F Street Club, for a dinner honoring the fiftieth wedding anniverary of a former secretary of the Treasury and his wife, Marty said it again.

"I know it began as a way to bring water to the people of northern New Mexico but in the process we may have found some things that make us too nervous not to fight the Bennett nomination—water or no water."

"Bushong already has a new brown Jaguar, if that's what you're talking about," Simmons said. "There's valet parking at this next place. I must get them to keep the car right there by the front door, though. What kind of car do you drive, Marty?"

"A BMW."

"I'd have a foreign car like you and Bushong if I could."

"They really don't cost that much more, sir."

"I could not drive a foreign-made car."

"Are there auto plants in New Mexico?"

"No, but there are a lot of Ford and Chevy and Chrysler dealers and their employees and damned few Jaguar and BMW dealers and their employees."

"Ford now owns Jaguar."

"You just don't understand politics, Marty. It's good you're into intelligence."

Into intelligence? Don't understand politics? Look here,

Senator, I'm on the road to a full and fruitful career in politics. I'm only doing intelligence now because it's my job. I *know* politics.

Marty said it all again, but straighter, as they made their way from the F Street Club to the Washington Hilton on Connecticut Avenue north of Dupont Circle for the annual fund-raising dinner for a Republican women's group.

"We have evidence Bennett really is a thief and a liar, Senator," he said. "A case could be made for his not being confirmed under any circumstances. A good case, a believable, nonpartisan case."

"We have a deal. I cannot go back on my word."

"This is important."

"My word is important."

"I didn't mean to suggest it wasn't . . ."

"The Washington Hilton here was where that kook shot Reagan," the senator said.

"I remember that," Marty said.

"There are so many hotels and so many differences among them. I've often wondered why, haven't you?"

Marty said he had.

On the way back to Capitol Hill after the Washington Hilton event Marty said it one more time.

"I believe you should do everything possible to deny confirmation to Joshua Bennett, sir. I believe the intelligence apparatus of our nation should not be in the hands of a man who steals and lies. I believe that these concerns supersede your personal concerns . . ."

"My concerns are not personal, Marty. Water is not personal."

"I understand—"

"Do you know what it's like not to have water?"

"No, sir."

"Enough said."

It was eight-ten, according to Marty's wristwatch, when they drove back into the Senate parking garage. They had left for event number one at six-fifteen. Four dinners and three receptions in one hour and fifty-five minutes.

"All in a night's work in behalf of the people and their business," said Simmons.

A few minutes later he left Marty with some final words: "I think the Ritz-Carltons are the best, although I know a lot of people who think the Four Seasons hotels are tops. I guess it's a close call. I don't know that much about it because we don't have either in New Mexico."

Jay Buckner's Civil War–era farm near Shepherdstown was called Belleau Wood, so named by the retired World War I Marine general who bought it in a falling-down state in the 1920s and brought it back to life. Charlie had been there a few times during the day but never at night. He and Jay did not socialize. The place had been designated an official Bicentennial Farm during the 1976 celebration year, an insignificant piece of information Charlie knew because it was emblazoned on a small red-white-and-blue sign that remained proudly in place out by the front gate.

"Come in, come in," Jay said. "I'm watching television is all. Nothing important."

There had been a scary several-minute wait before Jay answered Charlie's knock on the front door. The barking of what sounded to Charlie like at least a hundred dogs out there in the darkness somewhere had surely alerted Jay well in advance of the knock that somebody was around. There was no telling what more-exotic security devices a former tech man like Buckner also had at the ready. That bicenntennial sign, for instance, was probably wired to explode in the hands of any high school kid who dared try to steal it.

Charlie had elected not to phone in advance. He was in the Wagoneer on the way back from Sam's to Hillmont when he decided he had to discuss a very special mission with Jay Buckner.

And it couldn't wait.

The breakfast meeting was a sham. Senator Maloney opened with a monologue about the differences between late autumn here in Washington and back home in Maine. He described in detail the fun he had as a boy playing in great huge mountains of leaves at his grandparents' home somewhere south of Augusta. Then he asked Simmons what late autumn was like in New Mexico.

"It's really terrific," said Simmons. "Watching the evening sun go down in the west is like watching a moving piece of art."

Speaking of a moving piece of art, what about the hearing this morning? Marty was beginning to wonder if they'd ever get to it. Finally it did come up, but only at the very end, when all four of them were on their second cup of coffee and were about to go their various ways.

"Jack here says your questions for Bennett are tough ones," Maloney said to Simmons, in much the same friendly way he had asked about the late autumn in his state.

"I am hoping to get answers before I actually have to ask them," Simmons said, in much the same way he talked about the western sunset.

"I have every confidence that you will," said Maloney.

"So do I," said Simmons.

In other words, the Faucet would send word that the deal with the White House for the El Paso judge was set. Thus no need to proceed against Bennett, thus no questions, thus everything had worked out just the way it was supposed to.

Marty tried to engage Simmons in a discussion about it after they left the Senate dining room.

"Well done," said the senator to Marty.

"I urge you to consider the consequences of putting Bennett in charge of Central Intelligence—"

"You pulled it off."

"Sometimes there are matters that come up that require each of us in our own way to rise above—"

Simmons turned down a corridor into the waiting company of the timber and water aides.

Marty, alone now, walked down two flights of stairs and then outside into the late-autumn morning of Washington. It was only eight-thirty. There was an hour and a half before the Bennett hearings started again.

He turned to the north toward Union Station, where there were not only Amtrak trains to New York, Miami and all other points north, south and west but also many great restaurants, shops, movie theaters and other delightful diversions. Marty saw it as one of the few downtown rehabilitation-development projects besides Faneuil Hall in Boston that really worked, that was really fun.

It was only a fifteen-minute walk. He had no particular place in mind to go. He'd already had breakfast; most of the stores wouldn't be open yet so he would just wander. Windowshop. Think.

"I know you're too young to have been a fan of a radio program called *Grand Central Station.*"

Marty recognized the voice immediately. He did not have to even look up from the window of Brookstone, an upscale hardware-and-gadget shop, to know the person addressing him was none other than the old spook himself, Charles Avenue Henderson.

There he stood, smiling, his hands in his pockets—cool, relaxed.

"You know the truth," Marty replied. "I never even heard of such a program."

They moved closer and faced each other, as train passengers and others hurried by them on either side.

"It opened with the noises of steam whistles and chugs and porters and conductor shouts. There was a different story every week, each based on people who came into contact—usually by chance or accident—inside Grand Central Station."

"Sounds like something I would have enjoyed," said Marty. "Sorry I was born too late to hear it."

"You are living it as we speak, Mr. Madigan. You are in a

story about two people who came into contact by chance or accident inside a great railroad station."

"You just in from West Virginia, I presume?"

"You presume correctly. I hear your senator is really going after my friend this morning in a full-bore, go-for-blood attack. I hear he's got a peck of killer questions. True or false?"

A peck? Talk about old-fashioned, Marty thought. He said, "Yes."

"Yes?" replied Charlie, so proud of himself for pulling a word like "peck" out of his memories of grade-school arithmetic.

"Yes, it's either true or false. What else do you hear?"

"Nothing. I'll see you there."

Charlie took a step or two past Marty, but then Marty called for him to stop. Marty made a decision. Why not put this poor man and his friend out of their goddamn misery? Why not? The game was over. Why not tell all of the players?

"As a matter of fact, Mr. Henderson," Marty said, "my senator plans to ask no killer questions this morning. His bushel is full of nothing but softballs. Your friend will not be the subject any kind of attack. None of his blood will spill."

Charlie could not believe what this man was saying. "I have had some experience in the world of disinformation, Mr. Madigan. If that is what you are up to, I assure you it will not take."

"I am up to nothing but the truth." Marty spoke with directness, sureness.

Charlie, a professionally trained skeptic, read truthfulness in Marty's voice and body language. "A happy ending to this railway station story—thank you."

Marty watched Charlie walk away. Charlie met up with another man and continued to walk on toward the front door of the building. Marty did not recognize the other man.

"We win," Charlie said to Jay Buckner as they walked.

"Win?"

"Madigan says it's all over."

"Why?"

"Don't know, don't care."

"I smell a rat."

"Better than a fish."

"Will the committee please come to order," said Senator Maloney, banging his gavel on the table. The room became quiet, and Maloney looked down at Josh Bennett at the witness table. "Good morning, Mr. Bennett. I assume you come to us prepared but relaxed about answering our questions."

Said Bennett, "Prepared, yes, sir. Relaxed? Well, maybe not as much as I hope to be after this is over."

There was some light laughter in the hearing room.

"You will soon be out of this misery—if misery is the word," Mahoney said.

"It is a pleasure not a misery, sir. But even pleasure must not be overdone in order to be fully appreciated."

More light laughs and smiles.

Good stuff, thought Charlie from his position in the second row. The hearing room was only one-third filled. Obviously the lack of fire and excitement had turned off most of yesterday's full house, whoever they were. Charlie realized he was more visible up there, but he would have called even more attention to himself by sitting in the back like some kind of sinister loner.

Marty was in his regular position right behind Senator Simmons. He also noticed the smaller crowd—not only fewer spectators but only a handful of reporters. He recognized the regulars from the *Post* and the *Times* who covered intelligence matters. There were no network correspondents to be seen. He saw no radio or newsmagazine people either that he recognized. The show was over. There would be no blood on this hearing-room floor. Bennett was going to make it, probably with a unanimous committee vote and then by voice vote in the full Senate. No story.

Senator Maloney had the first round of questions. They were mostly softballs. Important softballs about the differing cultures in the CIA—the suspicion the covert-operations people have for the overt analysis people and such things— but softballs nevertheless. Maloney read them off a piece of paper, and Bennett responded as if he were reading from a piece of paper. Bennett promised to keep the Senate and House oversight committees fully informed of everything the CIA was doing. He vowed to run the Agency with "firm, hands-on hands" to make sure no employee or agent of the Agency ever did anything that was not fully legal and authorized. He promised to make sure that it would never again be possible for an Aldrich Ames to go undetected as a mole for Russia or any other foreign power.

The most interesting question, to Charlie, at least, was:

"Mr. Bennett, one of the skills of a well-trained, experienced officer in the clandestine service is to be different things to different people, to obfuscate, to dissemble—to, in fact, lie in the line of duty. How do you plan to guard against these people using those same skills in their work relationships with you and others in positions of authority?"

Josh's answer, in Charlie's view, was a masterly example of what the senator was asking about. Josh, speaking as if the words were memorized, said: "Senator, that is a terrific question. I thank you, sir, for giving me the opportunity to speak on this subject. I am a career intelligence officer. I have devoted most of my adult life to this career. There is nothing that offends and upsets me more than seeing my career depicted in movies, books and elsewhere as some kind of evil way of life. Your question grows out of that. Many well-meaning Americans, influenced by this outpouring of what I would call hate-CIA material, honestly believe that we are all liars, if not assassins, working in accordance with our own agendas, our own foreign policy, our own personal moral compasses. That is not true, Senator.

"Occasionally an employee of the U.S. Postal Service throws some second-class mail into the trash instead of delivering it. Occasionally an inspector for the Department of Labor's Occupational Safety and Health Administration overlooks an infraction of the hard-hat rule on construction sites. Occasionally a nurse at a Veterans Administration hospital slips home with a set of VA silverware or bedsheets. Occasionally an employee of the Internal Revenue Service takes a bribe from a generous taxpayer. Occasionally a mechanic in the Pentagon motor pool helps himself or herself to a government carburetor or spare tire. Occasionally a U.S. Navy officer misreads a radar printout and sends a missile on the wrong course. Occasionally deplorable things occur within the government of the United States. The Central Intelligence Agency is no different from other government agencies. The Ames case was a special and dispicable tragedy but there are, of course, other problems from time to time. Occasionally an employee or contract agent of the Agency loses control of his or her judgment, his or her faculties, his or her various compasses. I am sure that this will happen again in my tenure—if I am confirmed—as director of Central Intelligence. But I assure you, Senator, and all other members of this committee and of the United States Senate and all other citizens of this country that their intelligence service is not populated by killers, liars and other evil people lurking in the shadows, defying the law and the right. We are moral people, Senator. We are people who care deeply about our country and our work.

"I would ask that everyone hearing my voice right now please remember that there is another 'Occasionally' to be kept in mind. Occasionally an employee of the Central Intelligence Agency gives his or her life for this country. Twelve did last year alone. And they did so mostly unnoticed and in secret. Their families didn't even have the consolation of a large public ceremony.

"Please forgive me for going on the way I did, sir, but in this post-Ames environment it is important that my answer to your question be heard and understood."

A few of the people in the audience, including Charlie, broke into applause. Senator Maloney gave a halfhearted beat of his gavel and warned against public displays of reaction.

It made Charlie so happy and proud. It made him so grateful that he had done what he could to make damned sure the bad guys didn't get Josh. It made him pleased Jay had blown up Bushong's mahogany-brown XJ6 Jaguar. It made him feel as if he were twenty-one again, that the Chinaman was right about those magic years between sixty and seventy.

Yes, but what in the hell was the question? thought Marty. He also had a new admiration for Joshua Eugene Bennett. He figured Bennett probably had rehearsed that one in front of mirror a few hundred times and then waited for an opportunity to spew it out. But that takes wit and smarts. Good job, Bennett. You're going to do just fine.

Even if you did steal one thousand forty-seven dollars from your high school student government.

Even if you did steal unknown thousands from the taxpayers through the use of phony expense vouchers.

Even if you did kill a Czech defector and then lie about how and why it happened.

ELEVEN

Senator Simmons began his turn by asking the bland, harmless, routine questions Marty had written.

"There is always much confusion about how the Central Intelligence Agency is organized. Could you explain that organization, please, sir?"

The Agency was divided into four directorates, said Bennett. One for administration, one for science and technology, one for operations and one for intelligence. It is the operations directorate that does all of the covert intelligence gathering—the spying—as well as the covert operations. It is the intelligence directorate that does the analyzing. The science and technology people deal with satellites and similar things and the administration directorate hires, fires, pays the bills and runs the health care plan and the motor pool, among other things.

Bennett explained this in excruciating detail for almost fifteen minutes.

Simmons only occasionally looked at Bennett as he spoke and, from Marty's viewpoint behind him, appeared never to pay more than passing attention to the answer. Marty knew the senator had brought a water-policy briefing book with him to read during what he predicted would be "the down spots" in the Bennett confirmation proceedings.

Even Charlie had trouble following some of what Josh Bennett said. And it appeared to him that Josh himself was on the verge of nodding off while he spoke.

Simmons plowed on. "Much has been said in this post–Cold War world about the need for the CIA to become more involved in economic intelligence. What is your view of that, sir?"

Bennett's view, more than five minutes in the telling, was that there was no role for the CIA in offensive industrial espionage, going after the international competitors of American business in any covert way. But he did believe there were steps the CIA could take to help American business combat agents from other countries seeking to steal or compromise corporate or technological secrets.

"But I believe we should be careful as we proceed," said Bennett. "In the words of one of our officers that have been widely quoted in the media: 'I am willing to risk my life for my country but not for . . . ,' and he named a major U.S. corporation."

Simmons said nothing because, Marty was sure, he wasn't listening. General Motors, Senator! It's General Motors the guy was talking about.

Marty leaned forward, tapped Simmons's elbow and whispered into his ear, "It was General Motors the guy was talking about, Senator."

"General Motors?" Simmons said to Bennett. Light laughter again rippled through the now-almost-deserted hearing room. Only Charlie, Jay Buckner, who had returned from his walk, and about twenty other people were in the audience. Not even the *Post* and the *Times* reporters remained in the press corps. Maloney and Simmons were the only senators present. C-Span had the only working camera and outside microphone.

"I don't think it would be appropriate for me to confirm or deny the real name of that major American corporation," Bennett replied.

It was less than a minute later that one of Simmons's water aides entered the hearing room through the "Senators and Staff Only" door at the back. He handed Marty a note, nodded toward Senator Simmons and left the room. Marty handed it up and on to his senator without reading it.

Simmons read the note immediately and with motions that bordered on fitful jerks said something to Senator Maloney, who immediately banged the gavel and announced a ten-minute recess. Senate business, sorry, he said.

Simmons was up and headed for the back door within seconds. So was Marty because the senator had motioned with his eyes and hands and most of the rest of his body for him to follow.

Something was wrong. And it was serious.

That was all Marty knew when he entered another small private office somewhere down a hallway and around a corner.

The water aide, a man slightly older than Marty, did the talking, referring often to some notes he gripped in his right hand. "Robertson called me urgently. He said the White House backed off. It seems the president personally promised that judgeship to that other guy. They tried to get him to take an ambassadorship somewhere in Africa or Latin America but he won't do it. The Fifth Circuit Court of Appeals sits in New Orleans and he has a daughter, a son-in-law and three grandchildren who live in New Orleans. He is not interested in moving to some foreign country, and besides the president promised the judgeship to him personally, and he's pissed. Markel—you know, the White House guy—says the president doesn't believe the threat against Bennett is serious. The president, believe it or not, said something to Markel about watching the hearings on C-Span and they looked like a bipartisan lovefest to him. What's the problem?"

"The problem is that we have a president who has so little to do he sits around in the middle of the day watching C-Span, that is the problem," said Senator Simmons.

Neither the water aide nor Marty chose to comment on that. Marty, just standing there thinking about it for a split second, wasn't sure what he thought. Sure, there were better things for a president of the United States to do than watch confirmation hearings on television, but on the other hand, there were also one helluva lot worse things, too. A lot, lot worse.

"What do they want me to do?" Simmons asked.

"Draw some blood. They'll keep the president watching. You draw some blood."

"This is absolutely ridiculous," Simmons said. "But the people's business occasionally requires a taste of the ridiculous." He looked right at Marty and said, "Give me some blood questions."

"They are right here, sir." And Marty pulled them out of his briefcase and handed them to the senator.

"All right, it's to war we go," Simmons said. "Water, gentlemen. It's a war and it's about water."

Marty, as the others left the room, stayed back for a few moments and made a quick phone call to an angry woman in White Rapids, West Virginia.

Again, Simmons read verbatim the questions Marty had written.

"Mr. Bennett, where did you go to high school?" Simmons asked.

"In Westwood, Massachusetts, my hometown," Josh answered.

"Were you not president of your high school student body there?"

"I was, sir. Yes, sir. I was. Thank you for mentioning it. I chose not to put that in my official bio. My mother in particular thanks you, I am sure."

Some small alarm sounded in Charlie. Josh was answering Simmons's questions in a spirit of friendliness and openness, in fun. But Charlie could see something very different on the face of Senator Lank Simmons of New Mexico. This guy was on his way to somewhere else besides fun. He looked like a different person from the one who had left the committee room some fifteen minutes before.

"Was it not true that the year you were president there developed a problem over the student government's funds?"

Charlie was sitting to Josh's right, which meant he had an angled view of Josh from the side. He didn't have to see his old friend's face to know that something terrible was happening. Something awful was hitting the fan.

Charlie looked immediately up to the senator's table, past Simmons to Marty Madigan right behind him. He tried to catch the bastard's eye. The bastard's eye could not be caught.

"Where were those funds kept?" Simmons was asking Josh.

Josh's voice was very soft when he said, "It was some time ago, Senator. But I think it was in a bank."

"Wasn't it definitely in a bank account, Mr. Bennett?"

"All right, it was definitely in a bank account, Senator."

"Did you have access to that account?"

"Yes, sir."

At that moment Charlie got to his feet and slipped up to the table, as if he were an official and this was a perfectly natural thing to do. He handed a piece of paper to Josh as if it might be something concerning war and peace and the future of the free world as we know it.

Josh said to Simmons, "Excuse me a moment, Senator."

Josh made a big thing of opening the paper and reading it. He read it slowly. The room, Simmons included, remained perfectly silent as he did so.

"Senator, I am sorry. But something serious has arisen. Normally I would not interrupt such an important proceeding as this. But it is in fact something that must be attended to immediately. It probably will not take long. I know we have just returned from a break but if we might take another fifteen minutes or so it would be most appreciated."

Henderson, you bastard! thought Marty. He had started worrying as soon as he'd seen Charlie's very public delivery of the note. What are you up to, Henderson? Marty remembered Bushong's warning. These old men do not age like the rest of us.

Simmons had no choice but to turn to Senator Maloney and agree to another recess.

"What have they got, Josh?"

"I stole some money from the student government."

"How much?"

"All of it?

"How much?"

"One thousand forty-seven dollars."

"Jesus, Josh."

"Thanks, Charlie."

"Why?"

"Because I needed it. My dad had to have an operation. It's a long and very old story."

"How did you get away with it?"

"I didn't. I got caught. But the man who caught me—the principal—let me go because he trusted me never to do anything like it again."

Charlie and Josh then spoke for several seconds only with their eyes.

Yeah, Josh, said Charlie's eyes, and the principal was not quite right, was he? You did do it again as a grown man, stealing from the Agency on your goddamn expenses.

Thanks again, Charlie, said Josh's eyes, for protecting me and then stopping me. That money wasn't for me either, remember. My brother was going to die from drugs if I didn't get him out of Boston and into a rehab place.

Charlie broke the brief silence. "How did the Agency miss the school thing on the personnel checks years ago?"

"They didn't miss it. I told them about it. They checked it out with the principal. No problem, water under the bridge."

"And now here it comes. It's that bastard Madigan. He probably dug it up."

"With Bushong's help, no doubt."

"I am so glad we blew up that sunavabitch's Jag."

"Shut up, Charlie. I'm going to withdraw."

"What? Over a goddamn thing that happened thirty-five years ago?"

"Thirty-five years ago. There's obviously more than that. They're after me and they've got me. I don't want to be splattered all over the papers and television as Josh Bennett, the thief. Once a thief, always a thief. I wouldn't be surprised if they've got something else."

"Carla Avery?"

"Yes. And they're also probably going to raise Berlin."

"So what? We screwed up, that's all there is to it. Why won't they believe us?"

They were again in that small room they had gone to yesterday morning. They were alone. Not even the suits were there this time. But Charlie assumed they were not really alone. Although he had never read or heard about the bugging of rooms at the United States Senate, it could not be ruled out.

Josh made a move toward the door. "I'm going to call the president and say thanks but no thanks. Then I'll find Maloney and tell him I have suddenly remembered an old heart problem. Or I've just discovered that my mother was a French industrial spy and I feel that this might cause America to lose confidence in me. Something like that. Goddamn it, Charlie. I am going to be smeared and destroyed as a liar and a thief . . ."

Charlie had an idea. Only one. It was the one he came in with that morning on the train from West Virginia. All he had to do now was to find Jay Buckner—and convince Josh to hold on for a few more minutes.

"Let me try one more thing," he said. "You've come too far to fold now."

"No bombed Jags or anything like that?"

"I promise. You have nothing to lose. Stay here, Josh, for as long as you can. Then, when you have to go back in there, you find a way to ask Simmons a question."

"What question?"

"The only one that matters. The one we have been unable to answer. 'Why in the hell are you after my ass, Senator?'—or words to that effect. Don't do it, though, until I signal you. Keep an eye on me. Don't go until I say go."

"Charlie, what are you up to?"

"Trust me one more time, Josh."

Charlie had to go.

"The Brazilian came over to us and now lives in Independence, Kansas," Josh said.

"What are you talking about, for Christ's sake?"

"The Shredded Ralston Brazilian. I ran that records sweep. It turned out he loved the plays of William Inge, so the Agency gave him a new identity and got him a job teaching at a junior college in Inge's hometown in Kansas. They've got a lot of his papers and memorabilia . . ."

Charlie had to go.

"Take a tip from Tom," he sang.

"Go and tell your mom," Josh sang.

"Shredded Ralston can't be beat," they sang together.

"How much blood is the question, Marty."

"It's got to be a lot, Senator."

"Not a whole lot, I wouldn't think."

"Enough to make the point to the president that Bennett's in trouble."

"You can back up all of this?"

"I can. I have a witness about the expenses who is on her way in now from West Virginia."

"How do we even know for sure that the president is watching?"

"We don't. But we must assume he is."

"There's really no need to go all of the way, Marty. Remember, if this works, Bennett's still going to end up DCI."

"You've got to make the point, though, Senator."

"But if I go too far we have a wounded DCI. That's not good for the country."

"Water, Senator, remember this is about water."

"Thanks, Marty. How far? All the way to Berlin?"

"Yes, sir. We may have to go that far. I'm not sure we'd ever break Henderson, but the exercise would be good for him—and for the country."

"Henderson? Who is Henderson again?"

"He's that old man who was with that old fat man who was so insulting and disrespectful to you and to the United States Senate. He's gone—he died, I understand, with a liqueur in his hand—but I am sure Henderson is doing everything he can right now to keep this from happening."

"Who died? I am not following all of this. Keep what from happening?"

"Bennett bleeding on the floor."

"What could this Henderson do to stop it?"

"I don't know. I honestly do not know. But, remember,

he's one of those who blew up Bushong's car and his purple dot."

"Purple dot? What in the world are you talking about, Marty? I don't know anything about any purple dots."

There was a knock on the door of the small hidden office in which they had been talking. Marty opened it. The senator's water aide was there.

"Bennett has asked for a few more minutes. Maloney gave it to him," said the aide. "There's a rumor Saddam Hussein is moving the Republican Guards again—something like that. Bennett's got to see to it—something like that."

"Shit," Marty said out loud.

What are you up to, Henderson? he shouted to himself.

Watching Jay Buckner was going to be painful. Charlie tried to remember a comparable situation in his life. A time when he had to just sit and watch while somebody on his side did something stunningly difficult and dangerous with a great deal riding on the outcome. Something that could blow up into many terrible pieces right there before him.

What came to mind was an evening in the American Bar at the Savoy Hotel in London when a MI5 tech wizard posing as a waiter was detailed to get a hand inside a briefcase to determine secretly and with no fuss whether it contained a mechanical computer "spy." The briefcase belonged to a visiting Israeli inventor-scientist who had created a small device that could pick up the contents and calculations on any computer from miles away. Langley had word that the KGB had blackmailed the guy. He gives them the gadget and the Soviet government lets his mother, brother and sister-in-law in Moscow emigrate to Israel. Charlie watched as the waiter-agent spilled a vodka tonic on the lap of the Israeli, who was sitting at a small cocktail table with a man Charlie's side knew to be a Brit Socialist writer who dealt big-time in secrets. While others scurried to wipe up the mess the agent-waiter did the job. Charlie, from his vantage point across the room, saw the man's hand go into and come out of the briefcase. A few minutes later, back in the kitchen, the agent reported his finding to Charlie and two other MI5 men. There was nothing in that case except some papers, a loaded pistol and something that felt like a small travel alarm clock rigged by wire to something else. The agent said explosives were not his particular area of expertise but he knew enough to suspect that what he fingered at the other end of that wire was a form of plastique explosive. Charlie and the MI5 men went back out into the restaurant. The Israeli was no longer at the table or anywhere else in sight. The Brit writer remained. So did the Israeli's briefcase. It was still on the floor by the chair he had recently vacated. Again, Charlie only watched as the MI5 agent-waiter used a telephone call or some other ruse to get the writer away from the table while the other two MI5 men swooped by and picked up the briefcase. They got it outside into the bottom of a huge metal trash dumpster only a few seconds before it exploded. The bomb was not very powerful, no one was hurt and the whole thing was blamed on IRA terrorists. It was a few days later that Charlie's side was told by somebody in Tel Aviv that the Israeli, in addition to being an inventor-scientist, also did an occasional assignment for Mossad. This particular one was to eliminate the Brit Socialist writer because of his increasing dealings in behalf of the Syrians. The method chosen was a small bomb that would kill only the target and no others but in a style that would immediately be blamed on the IRA.

Now it was Jay Buckner he was going to watch do something that was equally difficult and dangerous.

Simmons didn't continue the line of questions on the high school bank account. Instead, from Marty's list of questions, he read: "What is the procedure for being reimbursed for travel expenses in the CIA?"

"Sir?" said Josh.

"How do you get paid back for what you spend when you travel?" Simmons ad-libbed. "It's a rather obvious question."

Careful, Senator, thought Marty. Play it nice and easy. Show no hostility. Take your time. Back off . . .

"The same way it's done everywhere, Senator. Receipts are kept and then turned in for reimbursement."

Easy does it, Josh, thought Charlie. Keep the tone civil. Keep it pleasant. You are here in a spirit of the new post-Ames candidness and openness. You are a dedicated public servant with nothing to hide . . .

"Have you always followed these procedures, Mr. Bennett?"

At that moment, Jay came through the "Senators and Staff Only" door in the back. He was smiling. And, dressed in a well-cut dark gray suit with a blue dress shirt and conservative wine-and-navy-striped tie, he blended naturally into the setting. He walked slowly, with the nonchalance of a man who clearly belonged there. Jay Buckner was good at what he did.

Charlie took a deep breath and held it.

Marty only glanced at the man who passed him. He looks familiar. Who is he? Must be one of Simmons's other aides. The agriculture aide? He should have gone through me, though. He shouldn't just walk in and interrupt things like this.

Jay leaned forward and began whispering in Simmons's left ear.

"Excuse me, Mr. Chairman," Simmons said to Maloney, looking at Jay with annoyance.

Marty could tell Simmons was as confused as he was over who this man was. What's going on? Who is this guy? What does he want?

Charlie was still not breathing.

Marty leaned forward to hear what was being said to Simmons by the intruding aide.

"You mother called, Senator. She has been watching this on C-Span. She said your hair looks terrible. She asked that we bring you this comb."

"Hey, get out of here," Simmons said. "We're doing serious business here."

Marty saw something in the man's hand. It was a comb. This guy is carrying a comb! The stupid bastard walked in here with a comb so the senator can comb his hair.

"I'm just following orders, Senator," said Jay.

"All right, all right . . ."

Senator Simmons grabbed the comb and swept it quickly through his hair and then angrily handed it back to Jay.

Charlie let out his breath.

Jay, still smiling and acting as if he did this kind of thing hundreds of times a day, stepped away and then moved back and out the door.

Marty watched him leave. Who is this guy? What kind of Senate-ego mentality would send somebody in here . . . Wait a minute. Wait a minute! There is something familiar about that guy with the comb. That's it—he's the man who was with Charlie Henderson this morning at the train station! Sunavabitch!

Marty looked out past Simmons to Charles Avenue Henderson in the second row. You old spook, what are you doing?

Charlie saw Marty staring at him. Stand by, Mr. Madigan. You lied to me. You told me you weren't after Josh anymore. Liars never win, Mr. Madigan. Stand by for some surprises . . . maybe.

"I am asking you, Mr. Bennett, if you have always followed the prescribed Agency procedures in the handling of your own expenses." Simmons said to Josh.

When working together in the Agency, Charlie and Josh had had several ways of communicating. Sometimes it was by hand signals, a technique that developed naturally from the fact that both had been baseball players in their youth.

Josh now moved to adjust his chair. In the process he turned his head almost imperceptibly toward Charlie. Charlie put the forefinger of his right hand to the tip of his nose. To a casual observer it would have seemed only that he had an itchy nose.

The message was: Now. Do it now. Go, boy, go. Steal second on the next pitch.

Josh then said to Simmons in his best nice-boy tone, "Senator, I wonder if it would be possible for me to ask you a question at this juncture?"

Charlie's body and soul went into a frozen state.

A question? thought Marty. Say no, Senator! You're the one who asks the questions, not him. Don't do it!

Marty leaned forward to say that out loud to Simmons, but he got there too late.

"Well, as you know, Mr. Bennett," said Simmons, "we like to see ourselves up here on this side of the dais as the ones who ask the questions, but certainly, go right ahead. But let's not make a habit of it, if that's all right."

It was clearly meant to be friendly-funny, but there weren't enough people left in the hearing room to quietly laugh or smile.

Josh, still ever so nice, said, "Senator, would you mind please, sir, telling me why you have pursued this line of questions with me? Why, sir, you appear to be involved in a negative posture toward my nomination?"

What is this? thought Marty. What in the hell is this man doing? Nominees do not ask senators questions like this! What is this? *Henderson!*

Charlie tried to imagine the sight of a particular light male fish making passionate love to a particular dark female fish. He tried to hope that it was good sex for both of them.

He tried to pray that the oil their love-making produced in the female and that found its way into the jar Jay Buckner took at two in the morning from the Agency lab behind the fisheries did indeed have the power to make people tell the truth. He tried to imagine droplets of that oil flowing down the hair on Simmons's head and passing on through to the scalp and finally into the brain. He tried to feel the power of that oil as it took hold of Simmons's mind and soul and forced the senior senator from New Mexico to speak the truth.

"It has nothing to do with you, actually, it has to do with water, Mr. Bennett, to be perfectly honest," Simmons said. "I am trying to create the impression that I am really after you . . ."

Maloney banged his gavel. Marty leaped up and put his hand over the microphone on the table in front of Simmons. "Senator, if I could see you for a minute? We have a national security emergency. Iraq has probably invaded Kuwait again . . ."

He helped Simmons up from his chair and escorted him out the back door.

Josh stole another look at Charlie. Charlie put both of his hands out in front of him, palms down. In baseball, it's the signal umpires use to show that a player is safe on base or at home plate.

TWELVE

Most years it would have been monumentally stupid to plan a big event like a swearing-in ceremony outdoors in November. But this was not like most years. Not in anyone's memory had there been such a moderate and wonderful deep autumn as this. It made perfect sense to do it all out here on the browning grass, under the leaf-shedding trees in front of the main CIA building.

Look at this glorious day! thought Charlie. A great omen for Josh's great future. Charlie had a seat, a reserved seat, five rows back from the stage on the left side. Sitting around him were mostly the Agency's current hierarchy, deputies and assistants in the various directorates. Some of them he knew from his day, but most of the faces were unfamiliar. There was one familiar face he knew he would not see—that of Russell Bushong. He had already cleaned out his desk and disappeared into a non-purple-dot world in his mahogany-brown XJ6 Jaguar. Jay Buckner was off behind Charlie somewhere. So were Sam Holt, Juan Galinda and Gene Duckworth. They had all ridden down from West Virginia this morning in the Wagoneer but had decided beforehand that it might be just as well if they did not sit together at the ceremony.

More luck for this lucky bastard Bennett, thought Marty, as he admired the weather and the scene. Normally this late in November it's either raining like hell or blowing colder than Siberia. This was not a normal November in any way whatsoever. Marty was in the third row on the right side, sitting with Jack Allen and other Senate and House staffers of the two intelligence committees. The Senate Intelligence Committee had ended up voting unanimously to confirm Bennett. So did the full Senate just twenty-four hours later.

Senators Maloney and Simmons were on the stage in the second row with the chairman and vice chairman of the House Intelligence Committee, the Speaker of the House, the Senate majority leader and their counterparts on the Republican side. In the front row with Josh were five former directors of Central Intelligence, Josh's wife, Joyce, the Bennetts' two teenage sons and the president of the United States.

Charlie, not accustomed to being this close to presidents, thought this one looked particularly happy and pleased to be

here this morning. Selecting Josh and then getting him confirmed quickly and without much more than a small blip was
something rare for this new president. Most everything else
the poor man had touched thus far in his young presidency
had gone sour. Just this morning the *Post* had had a story about
how his Commerce secretary, a black woman from New York,
had dated and maybe even cohabitated with a Black Panther
political commissar when she was in college thirty years ago.

"If ever there was a perfect fit between man and job this
is it," said the president now in his remarks. "Josh Bennett
was born to direct this nation's intelligence service and on
this day in November, surrounded by the deep orange and
purple and red splendor of this marvelous space under this
marvelously blue sky in Langley, Virginia, that destiny has become reality. The United States of America is better for it, I
know. And so is the entire world."

Leo Spivey was the only former DCI to speak. He said
on behalf of himself and the others who had also held this
important post that the stuff of ego often makes ordinary
mortals such as those who become directors of Central Intelligence believe the search for an adequate successor is
doomed to failure. No one can really do this job, not like I
did it, at least. Then along comes Joshua Eugene Bennett,
said Spivey, to destroy the whole premise. Not only can Josh
Bennett do the job we did, he can and will do it better.

Maloney spoke briefly. So did Simmons.

Simmons had survived his brief attack of fish-oil-
induced candor. He survived mostly because nobody much
was watching. The AP man and the three or four other reporters who were still there didn't pick up on what happened

and neither did any of the few who saw and heard it on C-Span. Marty had kept him back in one of those secret offices until whatever it was had passed. The president had been watching the opening salvo against Bennett and he saw enough to make the deal. Grover got his judgeship, the people of northern New Mexico got their water and all was well with the world of government and the United States Senate.

Josh was the last to speak. He closed with these words: "Here in this special warm November sunshine in the presence of the people I serve most, the president of the United States and the leaders of the Congress, and the people I love most, my wife and my children, let me say to all people everywhere that I feel the weight and mission and critical importance of my new responsibility. I promise no miracles. What I do promise is hard work, honesty, integrity and loyalty—loyalty to my beloved Agency and its people, my beloved country and its people."

Well done, my friend, thought Charlie. OK, Reynolds was right. You're no Leo Spivey or one of the other great ones but you'll be just fine.

Good words, Bennett, thought Marty. But you are still a thief and a liar and all of the good words in the world cannot change that.

There was loud and sustained applause for Joshua Eugene Bennett, the new director of Central Intelligence. He accepted it with waves to the audience. Everyone was asked to remain where they were for a few minutes until the president had left the area. Then as the crowd was dispersing Charlie decided he would make his way to the stage, shake Josh's and

Joyce's hands and maybe say a word of hello to Leo Spivey. Leo had been the best Agency boss Charlie had ever had, first as the man in charge of covert operations and later as DCI.

Marty just wanted out of here. He had accepted what happened. Had accepted the fact that nobody is perfect. He acknowledged that stealing student government money as a kid and falsifying travel vouchers and covering up that Berlin mistake are not monumental offenses against law and order. He understood about water and power and politics in the Senate of the United States. He was prepared to go about his business as the minority counsel of the Senate Select Committee on Intelligence in a professional manner. He was ready to put it all behind him and deal with the Central Intelligence Agency under Joshua Bennett in a straightforward and professional manner. He was even able to accept the fact that he did not get a purple dot for his license plate. But at the same time, he wanted to get in his car as quickly as possible and get the hell out of here. He had to think about his long-term work and personal future.

Andrea. It had taken five please-have-her-call messages and three days before he finally heard the voice of Andrea Bartlett on the other end of a telephone line. He announced that his Bennett ordeal was finally over. She seemed to have no understanding about what he had been through, saying the Bennett thing looked easy and unanimous. He told her what lay behind it was a very wild and hairy story that he'd be delighted to tell her all about at dinner. How about Sfuzzi again? Or maybe another swishy Italian place. La Tomate. Bice. Galileo?

She said she was wrapped up in a rewrite of the entire transportation bill—everything from gravel roads to super-trains. Your Republicans are even trying to privatize Amtrak again.

"It's *my* big ordeal, Marty."

"When will it be over?" he asked.

"No telling. You know how that goes."

So, not only no purple dot, also no Andrea.

Charlie saw Marty first. It would have been easy for Charlie to have stopped in the crowd, turned away and avoided any encounter. Something—simple, childish meanness, he was sure—made him keep walking directly toward Marty. We won, Mr. Madigan, we won. May I gloat for a second or two? Too late to grow up now. In the words of a Chinese philosopher . . .

"Mr. Madigan, I am surprised to see you here," said Charlie.

"I would have been surprised if you had not been here," Marty replied.

They did not shake hands.

There were several matters Charlie would have liked to ask this turkey. Such as why did you lie to me that morning at Union Station, Madigan? But most important, what was Simmons on the verge of confessing about what the opposition to Josh was all about when you stopped him?

Marty wanted to grab Henderson, clearly the youngest old man he had ever dealt with, by his sport-coat collar and demand to know what was on that comb. Or was it something else? What did you old farts do to Simmons? I thought all of that kind of crap went out with those bizarre assassination attempts on Castro.

He had to say something to Henderson. "Maybe they'll

give you an honorary and permanent purple dot now. God knows you earned it."

"What exactly is a purple dot, Mr. Madigan?"

Marty assumed that was another Henderson put-on. He ignored that and decided to ask one question—a less combative one—that had to be asked. "I'd love to know, just for the record, what really happened that day in Berlin."

"What happened is exactly what I told you happened, Mr. Madigan," Charlie said truthfully. "We made two serious and stupid mistakes—I missed the gun on the frisk and Josh meant to only wound the Czech but the guy moved and took a fatal shot."

"I don't believe you, Mr. Henderson," Marty said truthfully.

Marty was overcome with the urgent need to run away as fast as he could. He seldom cried or got sick but he suddenly felt that he might break into tears or vomit—or both.

But he took a deep breath and counted to five and the crisis passed. He said, "Have a nice day, Mr. Henderson."

"I am," Charlie replied.

Marty Madigan turned and slowly walked away.

Charlie found Sam, Jay, and the others waiting for him by the Wagoneer. He had one unfinished piece of business to transact with Jay Buckner.

Charlie had let it slide until now, until it was all over, until Josh had actually raised his right hand and sworn to uphold the Constitution of the United States as director of Central Intelligence.

Now it was time to confront Jay, right now, right after he dropped off the others, including Sam, who was already making arrangements to close down Rosebud Antique Toys and the fisheries facilities. Sam lived up on Chestnut Hill Road overlooking the Shenandoah a few miles west of Harpers Ferry. The house had a spectacular view of the river from one hundred yards above.

"How much of that oil did you end up putting on that comb?" he asked Jay once they started back down the hill from Sam's place.

"Quite a bit," Jay said. "I didn't want to take any chances on there not being enough."

"What did you do with what was left over?"

"I destroyed it."

"How?"

"Poured it down the drain in my kitchen sink."

"How can I know that for sure?"

"You can't."

"You could be lying."

"That's right."

"You realize how . . . well, lethally important such stuff could be in various hands?"

"I do. It could also make me rich overnight. No more selling real estate, no more selling anything."

"Goddamn it, Jay."

"Goddamn *you*, Charlie. I said I poured it down the drain. Believe it or not, that's that."

"Isn't it interesting how automatically we all do it?"

"Do what?"

"Assume everybody's lying."

They drove north toward Jay's farm in silence for almost ten minutes. As they approached the driveway and the fading Bicentennial Farm sign, Buckner said, "For the record, Charlie, I found out about those purple dots. They're for real. My old contact on the seventh floor said it was something Bushong and a few of his bureaucrat friends dreamed up to avoid having their cars towed. It works like a charm, I understand." Buckner explained exactly what they were and how the call-first, no-tow system supposedly operated.

"I'd have given anything for one of those—still would," Charlie said, thinking of the next time he took Mary Jane to eat in downtown Washington. "You didn't happen to pick up an extra one, did you?"

Charlie stopped the Wagoneer inside the front gate of the farm.

"I couldn't even get one for me, Charlie," Buckner said. "They guard them like jewels."

Charles Avenue Henderson, the retired warrior, again instantly assumed that Jay Buckner, the retired tech man, was lying.

This time he kept his assumption to himself.

Back on the road toward Hillmont a few moments later, Charlie could imagine coming across Buckner's Toyota Camry four-door someday outside the Martinsburg outlets or the Yellow Brick Bank in Shepherdstown.

And there in the lower-left-hand corner of its West Virginia license plate would be a bright purple dot about the size of a dime.

ABOUT THE AUTHOR

This is JIM LEHRER's eleventh novel. He has also written two books of nonfiction and three plays. He is the executive editor and anchor of *The NewsHour with Jim Lehrer* on PBS. He lives in Washington, D.C.

ABOUT THE TYPE

This book was set in Bembo, a typeface based on an old-style Roman face that was used for Cardinal Bembo's tract *De Aetna* in 1495. Bembo was cut by Francisco Griffo in the early sixteenth century. The Lanston Monotype Machine Company of Philadelphia brought the well-proportioned letter forms of Bembo to the United States in the 1930s.